Broken

By

Birth

By

Dr. Jeri Fink

and

Donna Paltrowitz

Photography by Dr. Jeri Fink
Cover and book design by Derek Murphy

Broken By Birth
Written By Dr. Jeri Fink & Donna Paltrowitz
Photographs By Dr. Jeri Fink
Book and cover design By Derek Murphy

Published By Book Web Publishing, LTD
Copyright © 2016 By Book Web Publishing, LTD
All Rights reserved

ISBN: 978-1-941882-05-4

To Ricky
and all our children

Check out more *Broken* books written by Dr. Jeri Fink:

Broken By Truth

Broken By Birth

Broken By Evil

Broken By Madness

Broken By Men

Broken By Kings

Broken: The Prequel

To Purchase books <u>click here</u> or in <u>Amazon</u>

1976-1993

Ayla

1

He was a few hours old and about to be thrown away.

Ayla shuddered. The baby shuddered.

She counted his fingers and toes. She touched his chest to make sure he was breathing and smoothed the caramel-colored down on his head.

"You're the prettiest baby in the world."

That's what good Mommas were supposed to say. Ayla wasn't going to be a Momma for very long, so she had to get everything right.

"You're beautiful," she added. "You'll have a very good life."

"Ten minutes," Mack's voice roared through the gloomy basement apartment. He sounded like a Harley revving up for a long trip. Sometimes, Ayla would remember the caramel-and-white colored feral cat she had found on the street. It was a beautiful creature but lost, just like Ayla. There was sadness in the cat's yellow eyes – no one wanted her but Ayla. Like no one wanted the baby in her arms.

Mack appeared, a shadow beneath the crooked, caged industrial light.

The air smelled subterranean – moldy, old, and mildewed. Eerie canned music reverberated through her head. A commuter train thundered nearby, passing the Freeport Long Island Railroad Station.

They lived in the basement of a crumbling house, behind a factory on Sunrise Highway, and a block south of the railroad tracks. The entrance was in the back, through a sagging fence that was once painted bright blue. A water tower hovered over them like a blue monster stealing the sky. Druggies lived upstairs – she never knew how many – there was a constant flow of people, coming and going, beneath the old white metal awning on the front door. The tenants sold and used everything from heroin to meth. Sometimes there was an eerie quiet; other times music was so loud it hurt her ears.

"Ten minutes," Mack said again, his voice threatening. "Me," Mack pointed to his chest, "not him." He lifted his right hand, curled three stubby fingers into a fist, extended his index finger, and raised his thumb in a simulation of a gun. Grinning, he aimed at the baby's head. "Click."

Mack turned away and everything swirled in hand-held camera action – dizzying distortions on a bigger-than-life screen. Ayla blinked. She was tired and sore, but alive. The day had passed in a blur of pain; a day she would never forget and a day she would never fully remember.

Mack was the answer – the only road out of the basement apartment.

Mack's arms and chest swelled with bulging steroid muscles rippling beneath a sleeveless tee. His thick jeans hung over steel-toed Dr. Martens embedded with shiny silver eyelets. Both arms were covered with tattoo sleeves ending in SS lightning bolts that shot up his neck. On his thigh, the lightning bolts pointed to his penis. The tee covered a shoulder-to-shoulder chest tattoo of a Nazi Iron Eagle, a swastika in its claws, and a blood red eye.

Ayla closed her eyes. She was mesmerized by Mack's Nazi Iron Eagle. What did it say about him? Often, after they had sex, she would lie naked in his arms and trace the outline of the tattoo with her finger. It was like playing with fire – tempting energies that stoked both guilt and excitement. Why would a grown-up man play Nazi? Why did it make her heart pound and her body ache for him?

"You hear me?" Mack snarled. He never yelled; always spoke in frigid monotones.

His voice shocked her back into the present. The Baby. Mack. *Click.*

"I hear you," she said quickly.

Ayla thought of her mother's favorite song. She softly sang two lines from Patty Smyth's ballad.

> *There's a reason why people don't stay who they are*
> *Baby, sometimes, love, it just ain't enough.*

2

It had been a long and painful day. Ayla replayed the events like a television rerun. The pain began slowly and then escalated into wracking contractions that hurt more than anything she knew existed. Mack fled when the hard contractions began.

He left her alone and terrified.

She was lucky. He didn't punch her or use his Dr. Martens to kick her belly. He didn't call his buddies to watch, or pull her hair until she cried. He just left.

Ayla didn't know what to do.

How do you have a baby? She remembered videos from high school health class – detailed views of women giving birth. But she wasn't a woman. Women had happy people at their bedside, Daddy dressed in green scrubs, smiling nurses, and approving doctors. Pink and blue teddy bears were everywhere.

"See how special it is to have a baby," her teacher always said when the videos were over. "When you're married, grown-up, and ready to be a parent, it can be the greatest joy in your life – one you'll never forget."

This was very different. Ayla wasn't in a hospital with doctors, nurses, machines, and happy people. There was no pink or blue anywhere. She was a kid alone in a dingy basement apartment. Panic took over. Tears coursed down her face. Fear drenched her in sweat.

What happens when a kid *has a baby? Am I going to die?*

Ayla closed her eyes and recalled the sign painted on the side of a trailer, set at the edge of Merrick Road in Wantagh. It had been there for years. She never noticed it until after Mack had unsuccessfully tried to beat the baby out of her. They were on his bike, zipping down the street, headed to Mack's favorite place, the lighthouse at Montauk Point. It was a long trip but Mack didn't care.

He loved the noisy absence of people and the surf pounding the rocks at the Eastern tip of Long Island.

They passed the sign on the way out, but it wasn't until the return trip that Ayla, in a rare moment of insight, memorized the number.

It was on the side of a large police trailer with a large printed telephone number.

You've hidden your pregnancy . . .
You couldn't let anyone know . . .
Now you have a baby – DON'T PANIC

Would they help her *now*?

She grabbed her cell phone and with trembling fingers, hit the numbers posted on the sign. It was hard to dial, her fingers didn't want to work, her body convulsed in contractions. She finally got it right. The cell rang through and Ayla heard a voice.

"How can I help you?"

"Please," Ayla begged. "I don't know what to do."

The voice was strong and gentle at the same time. "What's happening to you?"

"I'm having a baby," she choked. "I'm having a baby – and I don't know what to do."

"Take it easy," the voice replied. "Where are you?"

"I'm alone."

"What's your name?"

"Ayla."

"Go to a hospital, Ayla. Tell me where you are and I'll send an ambulance. They'll take you to Nassau University Medical Center or South Nassau Communities Hospital, whichever you prefer. You'll be safe. Doctors and nurses will take care of you."

It sounded so good – people to help her – not be afraid like in the videos at school. Ayla shook her head. The other questions leaped into her mind.

What about Mack?

What about their deal?

Their *done* deal?

That was more important than the pain *and* the consequences.

"He'll kill me," she shrieked, "and the baby. I'm sure. No one can know. I can't go anywhere."

"He won't kill you – he can't if you're in a hospital. You'll be safe and . . ."

"No. Noooooo." Ayla howled. "You don't get it. You don't get *him*. I have to hang up. I can't . . ."

"Wait," the voice stopped her. "Don't hang up. We'll do it your way. If you won't come in, I'll help you from here."

"I don't know . . ."

There was a sigh. The voice had heard it all. "We'll do it your way, Ayla. I won't tell anyone or call an ambulance. You can trust me."

"He'll kill me," Ayla cried again.

3

The memories consumed her. She had found the caramel-and-white feral cat behind the factory that pressed up against their backyard. She brought him inside and fed him milk from paper cups and chunks of chicken left over from fast-food dinners. Ayla named him Baby.

Mack hated Baby. He watched Ayla cuddle the warm, purring animal. She stroked Baby's fur and sighed. Mack glared at them, day after day. Suddenly, after two weeks, he grinned. The smile didn't reach his eyes.

"You like it?" Mack asked. "Baby?"

"I love it."

"Good. Now I'll teach you a lesson. Something you won't ever forget."

Ayla didn't know what to expect. How could Mack hate such a pitiful creature? Baby sensed something and crouched, narrowing his yellow eyes, preparing to pounce.

Maybe Mack had decided to love the animal?

Mack was fast. In one seamless motion, he seized Baby from Ayla's lap and slipped out his hunter combat knife strapped on his belt. He flipped Baby on her back and slit open the cat's belly. Blood spurted everywhere as the creature shuddered and died, never making a sound.

Ayla screamed until the flat glow in Mack's eyes stopped her.

"I have power over life and death," he said tonelessly. "Your life and your death. Don't ever forget it."

He left the apartment, tossing the dead cat into an overflowing metal trash can, along with the resident roaches and marauding rats. Ayla cried for a long time, careful that Mack never saw her tears.

The apartment reeked of blood for weeks.

4

"Are you there, Ayla?" The voice jarred her back into the present.

"He has power over life and death," Ayla cried. "I know."

"We'll do it your way." the voice said again. "I believe you. I won't tell anyone or call an ambulance. You can trust me."

"Okay," she whispered. "I won't hang up."

"You promise?"

Ayla debated whether she should trust the voice. There was no one else. She desperately needed help.

"I care about you and the baby," the voice added.

"Thank you," she whispered, forcing Baby from her mind.

Her voice trembled. She bit her bottom lip until droplets of blood stained her chin. What kind of man cared about her well-being? Was he tall and gentle or short and stubby? Did he have a home full of children or was he alone with television and beer? What did he get from it? Was he a guardian angel or a pervert getting off on her pain?

Did he kill cats?

Ayla listened to his breathing.

A voice I always wanted to hear. Daddy's voice.

Another contraction hit. She didn't want to scream – she wanted to be brave and strong like Mack. Ayla was afraid that the druggies upstairs might hear. What would *they* do?

"Who are you?" She wailed. "Why do you want to help?"

5

He told her his name.

Ayla never heard it because he spoke during a contraction. She would wonder what his name was for the rest of her life.

"Listen to me," the voice continued calmly. "Do what I tell you and we'll get both of you through this."

Both of us? Ayla had never thought about her *and* the baby.

"I'm scared," she gasped. "You don't know."

"I do know. Just listen. The first thing you need to do is put your cell phone on charger so you don't lose power."

She struggled to her feet and followed his instructions. The charger stretched across the mattress into the single outlet. It took her several minutes to attach the wire, panting with each movement. When it was completed, she collapsed back onto the mattress.

"Now take a deep breath, close your eyes, and listen to my voice."

"I can't. I can't move or . . ."

"You have to – there's no choice."

Reluctantly, Ayla obeyed.

"I want you to find towels, washcloths, string, a scissor, and something to wrap the baby in."

"Yes," Ayla clenched her teeth. There were only a few frayed towels and rags piled on a crate. That was easy. She gathered them, struggling with each step. The string was closer to the door. It was stained from something. Ayla didn't want to guess. Mack used a lot of string, although she never knew why. She wouldn't dare ask.

Ayla stacked everything in a heap next to the bare, stained mattress. She reached beneath and pulled out a carefully folded, red-checked tablecloth stolen from *Pizza Baas*.

"Done," she gasped. "Will it ruin the mattress?"

"Probably. We'll worry about that after."

After?

She and Mack on the Harley, racing past ocean surf, through lush forests, and into frenetic city intersections. Together, just the two of them. No baby. No pain.

Another contraction hit. Was there going to be an *after*?

"I'm going to die!" Ayla wailed.

The voice soothed her. "This is natural – you're not going to die. You'll be fine. It will take time and then the pain will be gone. You and your baby will be safe."

Ayla responded with a scream.

Would anyone upstairs hear? Would anyone care? If Mack knew . . . Ayla stuffed her mouth with a rag to deaden the sound.

"He won't hear you," the voice said as if reading her thoughts. "I'll stay with you the whole time."

"How do you know?"

"I've done this many times. Mack isn't the first snake to let his girl go through this alone." The voice turned acid for a barely perceptible instant. "He won't be the last."

"You're wrong. You're wrong because Mack is good; he loves me and wants to take me away."

Ayla couldn't finish. The contractions pummeled her worse than when Mack beat her, as if the thing inside wanted to tear her to shreds.

"How often are they coming?"

"All the time."

"Can you count between the pains?"

Ayla struggled with the request. "A few minutes, I think."

"Good. You're going to be fine," the voice added. "I'll make sure of that."

"I don't know," she gasped.

"I *do* know. Women have been doing this since the beginning of time. You're going to be okay. You have to go with it, let your body and baby take over. Don't fight it, Ayla. Everything will work out."

Ayla had no choice. She couldn't stop what was happening to her.

6

It felt like years.

The voice guided Ayla through the hours, telling her what to do, when to push, and how to deliver the baby. He told her about the placenta and how to tie the cord with string and cut it with the scissor. The voice was unruffled by her screams; reassuring her that everything would be fine. He led her across time like a voice from heaven storming through hell.

Her guardian angel.

Ayla had never experienced such fear or pain in her life.

"Push," the voice said. "Push hard, keep your knees up, and catch the baby as it comes out."

Ayla obeyed through eyes glazed with tears and cracked, bitten lips.

Then it was over.

"It's a boy!" Ayla cried.

She stared at the baby on the mattress. It was sticky, messy, and ugly but it was a baby – a human life. Ayla tried to make sense of the thing lying between her legs. How did he come from her? Were the kicks and pokes from her belly now exposed?

She couldn't speak.

"Are you ok?" The voice asked.

"A boy," Ayla whispered, her voice thick with awe. "I made a boy."

The voice chuckled. "You sure did, Momma."

The baby began to cry. He screamed angry, hurt wails that made Ayla tremble.

"What do I do?" she asked, covering his face. "If Mack hears he will . . ."

"That's a good cry. You want to hear that."

"It doesn't matter."

The voice got it. "Hold him against you and don't cover his face."

"I can't," Ayla was terrified. "I have to quiet him."

"You will," the voice assured her. "Hold him in your arms against your breasts. He needs to know you're there."

"I . . ."

The voice was firm. "Do it."

Ayla wanted to run from the screams – stop the ear-splitting anger. Instead, she obeyed the voice, picked up the slippery, naked baby and held him against her skin. He nuzzled her breasts like Mack. Instinctively, she rocked him and discovered words she had heard long ago from a past she could only faintly recall.

Ahhhhhhh baby.

Ahhhhhhh baby boy.

It felt good. His skin was warm and a strange, primitive sensation spread through her. Ayla was comforted by the naked baby. He felt right. He stopped crying.

When the baby was quiet, the voice said gently, "wrap him in the cloth."

Ayla nodded as if the voice could see her.

"You're doing fine. See how you comforted him? Just like a good Momma. Now wrap him in the cloth to keep him warm but make sure you see his face. You don't want to cover his face."

She wrapped the baby in the red checked tablecloth. He was like a doll. Ayla rocked him in her arms.

"What next?"

"I want you to listen carefully. Go to a Safe Haven. Your baby will be fine. No one will hurt either one of you and no one will ask questions."

"Are you sure?"

"Yes, I'm sure. I've done this many times. It's state law and no one will hurt you as long as the baby is fine."

Ayla nodded. She didn't want to hurt her baby and she didn't want to hurt herself. Most of all, she didn't want Mack to kill either one of them. Ayla just wanted everything to go away – return to being a teenager, madly in love with her Nazi Iron Eagle Knight, and ride off on his two-wheeled black stallion.

"As soon as he gets back," she agreed. "Mack will go to Safe Haven. No one will get hurt."

Ayla took a deep breath and snuggled her baby.

"I can still send an ambulance right now, before he gets back. You and your baby will be warm and safe in a hospital. You'll be able to think things through . . ."

For a moment she hesitated. She heard Mack's voice in her head.

Done, Ayla. Done.

"No. No. No one will get hurt."

"Ok Ayla," the voice said gently. "Don't wait. Get Safe Haven for both of you."

"I promise." She meant it. "Thank you. I'll never forget you."

"Ayla . . ."

She cut the connect. "I'm sorry," she said out loud although the voice couldn't hear. "I'm really sorry," she said to the baby although he couldn't understand. The words came back unbidden.

Baby, sometimes, love, it just ain't enough.

Ayla would hold the baby, nuzzle the baby, kiss the baby, and for a small moment in time, she would love the baby. She was young enough and old enough to know that it wasn't enough. The baby needed a real life – a Momma *and* a Daddy, with two people to love and protect him.

I need Mack. Only Mack.

The choice, made so many times during the last few weeks, was confirmed. The road she would travel was with the father not the son. The son had to find his own way.

"I'm sorry," she whispered into the baby's ear. "So very sorry. Just remember that I once loved you."

Could a baby remember that?

Did it matter? Ayla's daddy had never loved her and she grew up. She squared her shoulders and closed her eyes. The baby would grow up, too.

7

Mack returned to the basement apartment. He made a lot of noise parking his Harley, locking it up, and clamoring down the steps. The door flew open like a cop raiding a drug den. If it was TV, people would scream, scatter, and leave unfinished drugs on the floor.

It was only Ayla and the baby.

Mack stared at her coldly as she and the baby lay on the soiled mattress. Ayla's eyes fluttered and she saw him hovering above them. Her heart raced.

He snarled.

"Are you going to hurt us?" She whispered.

"Ten minutes."

Mack shook his head, a growl in his throat. Ayla's hands trembled. The dead cat raced through her mind. She heard his voice, echoing through her head like a musical score from a horror film.

Now I'll teach you a lesson.

"Hear? Ten minutes." Mack barked. Grey hair fell across his forehead, matching the stubble on his face.

Ayla was too tired and sore to withstand Mack's beating. She knew that if he had the chance, Mack would kill the baby, and maybe her, too. Mack had killed before. It would be easy. All he needed was his precious hunter combat knife and he slit their throats. The baby, small and unable to resist, would be faster. Then he would leave them behind, dead, until they smelled up the basement apartment and someone called the cops. The rats and roaches would pick at their remains. By the time the cops and Medical Examiner arrived, Mack and his gang would be half-way across the country.

Ayla clutched the baby and blinked her eyes.

"Ten minutes," she whispered, not meeting his eyes. "We have a deal. I won't back out. You promised."

What did a promise mean to a man like Mack?

Mack grunted. "I'll take it to Safe Haven. Like we agreed. And then we're outta here." Mack turned and was swallowed by shadows.

"I won't kill it," Mack called over his shoulder.

That was the promise. The baby would live and she would head west with Mack.

"I'm sorry," Ayla said to the baby. "I only have ten minutes, but I'll love you with all my heart for that time."

Ten minutes, Ayla thought. Ten minutes to say goodbye. Ten minutes to be a Momma. Ten minutes to study her son, memorize his cry, touch his soft skin, and cuddle him as if they were spending the rest of their lives together.

After that it was over. Mack came first.

Ayla loved Mack with all the passion of an angry teenager. He was her life, not this baby. She and Mack would ride off into the sunset, lost in a cloud of biker dust, plunging into adventure, excitement, parties, and love . . . forever. That was the story and happy ending.

There was another piece. She and Mack *and his biker gang* would be together, forever. The hairy, grunting men she serviced when Mack demanded. Mack owned her and lent her out to reward his underlings. They worshipped him and he gave them what they needed. Ayla didn't like it but Mack told her she had no choice. She had to do what he demanded.

Ayla pleasured them but never fucked them.

"That's only for me," Mack told her, his voice threatening.

She obeyed. Except now there were two men who owned her privates. Mack and his son. They belonged to her and she belonged to them; forever linked.

Ayla took a deep breath and nuzzled the baby. They were heady thoughts, too cumbersome for her young, tired mind. Think of the moment. The baby, Mack, the voice on the phone . . .

She sighed. He felt so right in her arms. He was a part of her story, even for only ten minutes. It was a story alive with secrets and predators; a tale she never really knew until her 16th birthday and Moeda came clean. It was a story of power and money; predators and prey.

She sighed and ran the awful movie in her head.

8

Ayla's mother loved their home. She saw colors and brush strokes that weren't there. One day she bought a set of expensive oil paints, a large canvas and easel, and created a pink and purple painting. She was so proud of her work that she hung it, gallery-like, in their front room.

Ayla hated it.

Ayla and her mother lived in a small, California Spanish Stucco home with a turret, in The Gables Estates. It was a tiny community-within-a-community, lying in Merrick, Long Island where the houses were built for people who had money to spend.

Their lives weren't the colorful dabs of purple and pink oil paint on a canvas. It was more like a greyscale – black to white and everything in between. Like her name. She insisted that Ayla call her Moeda in a throwback to relatives from 17th century New Amsterdam. Moeda refused to be known as Ayla's Mommy.

"It's a Hollywood thing," Moeda explained.

She changed the spelling from Moeder to Moeda because she thought it was cool. That was very important in 1976 when Ayla was born and Moeda was still a teenager.

Moeda never knew that Ayla hated the painting. She didn't know much about her daughter at all.

"The art has meaning, dear. Our home is very special," Moeda explained, over and over again.

The stucco house had been built in the 1920s, designed to look like the homes in Hollywood at the time.

"Some people claim," Moeda smiled mysteriously, "that the neighborhood got its name from the legendary Clark Gable."

Ayla never heard of Clark Gable.

Over the years, The Gables changed, additions were added, fancy landscaping put into place, and expensive cars parked in the driveways. Taxes and property values skyrocketed.

"It's never lost the *look*," Moeda bragged.

Inside, everything looked like it was plucked from a YouTube video; classic Americana – distressed wood, floral fabrics, wood decoy ducks, fake wildflowers, and roughly carved boxes. A tacky painting of midwest cornfields swaying in oiled winds hung above the couch. Sometimes Ayla stared at the painting and found tiny figures lost in the stalks.

Ayla hated that painting as well.

Moeda treated Ayla more like a best buddy than her daughter. There was always money to go shopping, buy expensive food, take fancy spa vacations, and just about anything they wanted. Ayla had the best stuff – pricey dolls when she was a little girl, fancy electronics, and designer clothes as a teenager. Moeda never said no.

Ayla went to a private Long Island school with tuition higher than many incomes. Moeda claimed she paid the tuition with the money she earned from her "art." She had made a small painting of the Montauk Point Lighthouse and copied it onto refrigerator magnets, ceramic tiles, and metal key chains. On the bottom she wrote *Long Island, New York*. They were sold in local souvenir stores.

The gig was like a bad sit com. The money Moeda made from her 'artwork' wouldn't pay for the cleaning lady.

The real money came in the mail – a check on the first Monday of every month. Moeda grabbed the envelope and slid it into her $1,000 *Prada* tote. Ayla asked questions about the check, but Moeda refused to answer. Once, Ayla opened the envelope before Moeda. It was a simple bank check. No name, no note. The number was staggering.

Where did the money come from?

After that, the checks stopped. Direct deposit. Moeda made sure there was nothing for Ayla to see.

The money was another clue in the mystery.

How do we live? Who sends the checks? Where is my father?

The answers always changed. She knew there was a father somewhere. Ayla looked like him. Moeda was olive-skinned with thick, curly brown hair and dark eyes, while Ayla had silky, caramel-colored hair and blue eyes. Whenever she asked about her father, Moeda lied.

"Your father is dead."

Ayla guessed that the check came from him so Moeda revised the story.

"He's an undercover agent with the CIA."

Ayla figured that a government spy couldn't afford the money.

"He's a wealthy businessman in China."

"A Navy Seal hostage in the Middle East."

"An international banker in Switzerland."

He was anything or anyone that Moeda could conjure – dramas that never rang true. So Ayla wrote her own story.

Daddy was a hero. His courage was known throughout the underground world. Daddy's job was to rescue important people from the flames of evil, and spread justice across the planet. Moeda and Ayla were *his* secret. He protected them by staying away – a witness protection program for the brave and righteous. Daddy loved Moeda and Ayla so much that he gave up his right to see them to assure *their* safety and happiness.

Just like TV.

Moeda didn't care – she wanted the money, but when Ayla turned 16 their lives unraveled.

Moeda bought a tiny, expensive cake to celebrate, decorated with frosting roses. She placed 16 candles plus "one to grow on" on the top. Ayla stared at the candles. What did it mean? What was her future? How could she understand anything when her past was filled with Moeda's lies?

There was no special dinner, party, gifts, or friends. There were no sisters, brothers, aunts, uncles, or cousins. It was Ayla and Moeda. It had always been just Ayla and Moeda. Ayla stood in front of the cake and 17 fiery candles.

"Make a wish," Moeda slurred, balancing her fourth glass of 2008 *Chassagne-Montrachet* table wine. "I'm recording everything so you'll never forget today or your 16th birthday."

She raised a new, expensive video camera and aimed it at Ayla and the birthday cake.

Ayla glanced at her mother, hesitating to blow out the candles. She gave her mother a strange look, her eyes questioning. Why did Moeda need wine to celebrate? What was so important about this birthday? They had never really celebrated the ones that came before.

"Make a wish," Moeda repeated. "A good one. You'll need it."

Ayla had only one wish. It was the same wish for as long as she could remember.

Who and where is my Daddy?

Ayla closed her eyes and repeated it mechanically, resigned that it would never come true.

"This year it may come true."

Moeda's words startled Ayla. She opened her eyes, looked at her mother, and the candles flickered. A single drop of sweat wound its way down the side of her face and onto the frosting.

"What?"

"Blow out the candles," Moeda said in a voice Ayla didn't recognize.

Ayla never blew out the candles. She stared at her mother instead.

"Come with me."

"Why?"

"Don't ask, just listen."

Ayla didn't like it. Something strange fluttered through the puffy curtains.

They never ate the cake. The candles melted into an ugly blotch on the frosting. The cake would remain untouched until Moeda threw it in the garbage, three days later.

"Sit," Moeda said, pointing to the overstuffed couch in front of the large TV.

Ayla stared at her.

"Sit," Moeda said again. "You're 16. It's time."

"Time for what?"

Moeda didn't answer. Ayla sat on the couch, sinking into the cushions. Moeda sat next to her, picked up the remote, flicked on the TV, and started the VCR.

"I have something to show you."

It was a report on a political fundraising event.

"I don't understand."

"Sssssh," Moeda said heavily. "Just watch."

The President of the United States stood behind a podium emblazoned with the Presidential Seal. He was telling a political anecdote that had little meaning to Ayla.

"Why do I have to watch *him*?"

"Sssssh." She took a deep breath and began slowly, her voice drifting from an old and rusted place. "I was a kid. The same age as you. Sixteen. I was a smart high school kid with a lot of ambition. There was a competition to become a congressional aide and I won."

Ayla had never heard this story.

Moeda didn't look at her. She focused on the screen. "I believed. Do you understand? *I believed.*"

Ayla was confused. Moeda rarely talked about her youth.

"Watch."

Ayla turned to the screen. The President concluded his speech by introducing The Senator, who was sponsoring the fundraiser. The Senator shook the President's hand. The President hugged The Senator's wife, a well-dressed older woman who carried herself with stiff dignity, the young adult daughter who looked uncomfortable with the attention, and her fraternal twin who grinned unabashedly into the camera. The audience cheered, the hall reverberated with patriotic music, cameras flashed . . .

"Who cares?" Ayla asked impatiently.

The commotion settled. The Senator took the podium. He wore an expensive suit and expertly worked the cameras.

"Thank you Mr. President," The Senator said, flashing his famous smile. "Thank you. Thank you. Thank you." He opened his arms to the audience. "A warm thank you to my wife and the twins

– Kiran and Robert. I'm so pleased you joined us today. This is a great time for families to love and support one another." He beamed at his children and wife. They obediently returned his smile. He took a deep breath and cleared his throat as if momentarily overcome by emotion.

The Senator bowed his head for three seconds of television humility. "Our President has honored us with *his* family as well." The Senator had blue eyes and caramel-colored hair.

Ayla turned from the TV to Moeda. Moeda wouldn't look at her.

"In these days of crumbling families, illegitimate children, abandoned babies . . ."

The voice drew Ayla back to the screen.

"He leads the U.S. Senate Subcommittee on Children and Families" Moeda mumbled bitterly. "That's what he's known for . . . family values."

"We have to band together," The Senator continued. He took a deep breath and stared at the camera with heroic intensity. "We must establish a solid, unbreakable front that tells the world we're all part of the same family . . ."

There was polite applause.

"We have to support family values, not turn away from our children. Fathers have to honor their responsibilities . . . children come first."

"Why are you making me watch him, Moeda? On my 16th birthday?"

"It's time you know the truth."

"I don't understand."

"I was so happy when I found out I was pregnant," Moeda said. "I knew he would leave his family. I was pretty and young. His wife was 49 – an old lady. I would be the new political wife, support his campaigns, follow him around the state, and be best friends with his kids . . ."

Ayla couldn't make sense of what Moeda was saying. A congressional aide – The Senator's wife – his kids' best friend? Ayla's head filled with fragile thoughts like a Dandelion Puffball, ready to explode and spread its soul in a million different directions. She struggled to sort out what she was seeing and hearing. It refused to come together and form a single coherent thought, as if the wind blew in to scatter the puffball.

9

Moeda was silent, lost in her past. She closed her eyes. Ayla stared at her, heart pounding, wondering what her mother was trying to tell her.

"I was so young," Moeda said finally, her voice in a distant place. "He said wonderful things. He told *me* wonderful things." She mimicked the words. "I wanted you since the first moment I saw you. Your beauty outside only matches your beauty inside. You make me dizzy with desire."

Moeda's eyes were glassy.

Ayla could hardly breathe.

"I was so young. What did I know? *I believed . . .*"

"Family values," The Senator's voice droned from the television.

"We would make love," Moeda smiled, "crazy, wild love. He took me to places that I never knew existed. When we finished he'd smile and say 'Thank you. Thank you. Thank you.' I thought it was so cute – boyish for such a powerful man. I never guessed that it was a skillfully executed performance."

The voice from the television was a buzz in Ayla's head.

"It was a beautiful night when I told him," Moeda continued. "I had everything planned. We made love in his office as usual. On the floor, the way he liked it, after hours when everyone was gone. We had the building to ourselves. I did everything he wanted and when we finished he held me gently, lovingly. Then I told him."

Ayla hung on to the slippery words.

"I was pregnant."

Ayla froze.

"I thought he would be happy, hug me, kiss me . . . he slapped me across the face. Hard. He slapped me again, his eyes icy, as if he had shed his mask of charm. Then he called me a fucking kike."

Ayla gasped.

"Funny," Moeda shook her head. "I'm not even Jewish."

Ayla didn't know what to say.

"He kicked me, cursed me with words that chilled my soul. I had never seen that part of him, as if he had cleverly concealed everything, showing only what he thought I wanted to see. I was terrified."

Moeda continued as if unaware that Ayla was listening. "He said that I had to get rid of you – my baby – before you ruined his life."

Red, orange, and yellow swirled through Ayla's head. She fought to put things together and clear the fire.

Get rid of me?

"I wouldn't do it," Moeda frowned. "I could never do it. He told me that if I agreed to stay quiet – if no one ever found out – he would arrange to send me money. A lot of money. It would keep me and you comfortable for the rest of our lives as long as I stayed quiet." She paused. "*I believed.*"

Moeda's voice hardened as she stared at the face on the screen. "He's a very rich man. Money and power run in his family."

"You let him pay you off?"

The television screen suddenly caught their attention. Ayla and Moeda turned to watch.

"Family reigns supreme," The Senator roared to his audience, raising his arms in victory. "Thank you. Thank you. Thank you." He smiled.

No one could resist The Senator's charm.

The applause was thundering. People jumped to their feet as The Senator pulled his wife and kids into camera view, his arms draped over their shoulders.

Moeda moaned. "He's evil," she whispered. "No conscience. No empathy. No remorse." Moeda ran the words together like a column of numbers. "He has no feelings." She paused, as if that was his greatest crime. "He told me to take the money and run. If I went public he would deny everything, fix the paternity test results, make sure that I was penniless, alone, and with a bastard kid."

Moeda took a deep breath that rattled like pebbles in her chest.

"The easiest way was to get rid of it. *You.*"

Ayla twisted her fingers together until the knuckles turned white.

Did I come so close to death before I was even born?

There was frozen silence. The TV shifted into slow motion, the cheers from the crowd became a low growl. Everything faded but Moeda's words.

"It was *you* Ayla. I could never get rid of you."

The President hugged The Senator. He hugged The Senator's wife and children. In a flourish of music, The First Lady glided onto the stage, followed by her children. The roar was deafening. Even the reporter who tried to speak directly into his microphone couldn't be heard.

"Me," Ayla whispered, her heart pounding. "The Senator's *daughter*?"

"You. I ran away from home. I refused to talk to my parents or anyone else in my life. *I was humiliated.* How could I reveal what happened? How could I tell them about The Senator? I fled with The Senator's money and holed myself up . . . here. My mother would have forced me to have an abortion, but I wanted you too badly. I never spoke to my family or friends again." She took a deep breath. "I wrote to my parents and told them to leave me alone – I was gone – dead in their eyes. They tried to find me . . ." Moeda shook her head. "You can hide in plain sight. Do you know what I mean? Once I saw someone from my old neighborhood, far from home, and she recognized me. I walked right past her, pretending I didn't know her. *I deleted my family.* That's why you never had grandparents, aunts, uncles, cousins. That's why we spent the holidays alone, just the two of us."

Ayla's mouth dropped.

I have a family. Somewhere.

"I made a promise to myself and you," Moeda continued. "When you turned 16, I would tell you the truth."

Ayla stared at the screen – at *her* face reflected in The Senator. All the fantasies, lies, and stories crashed. He wasn't a hero – a courageous man whose mission was to rescue important people from heinous fires and battle the flames of evil, determined to protect his family from danger. He didn't give up his right to see them in order to protect her safety and happiness.

He made a business deal so we would go away forever.

Politically correct. A politically correct snake.

Moeda waited. The blue eyes and caramel-colored hair on the screen were the same as Ayla's. Genetics never lie.

Something ugly rose in Ayla's throat.

I want to die.

Moeda took her hand but Ayla pulled it away.

I want to die but I won't let him kill me.

Something hardened inside Ayla – dark, cold, and fed by inconsolable rage.

A primal cry materialized. Ayla ran. She ran from the California stucco house and Americana décor; she ran from her mother's tears and excuses. She ran through the streets of The Gables Estate, past meticulous landscaping, expensive cars, and old, perfectly groomed trees. She ran south and then west onto bland Merrick Road where the cars, whizzing by, didn't care. Ayla ran until her body was bathed in icy sweat, her hair tangled, and her eyes burned with rage. When she couldn't run anymore, when her breath felt like shards of glass, she sat on a bench at Cammanns Pond and watched the night creep like black ants over the water.

A lone goose watched with her. They were the same creatures, abandoned by their worlds.

Ayla struggled to think. There was nothing in her head but five ugly words.

I was sold for money.

Hours later, Ayla returned home because she had nowhere to go. Moeda sat on the couch in the same place, her eyes red and swollen. The television screen was black. Ayla paused. The two women glared at one another. Moeda stood up and opened her arms.

Ayla shook her head and backed away. She hardened her eyes, tossed her hair over her shoulders, and turned her back. No words were spoken. The image of the goose at Cammanns Pond was burnt into her mind. There was no going back.

10

The next day Ayla cut school. She walked along Sunrise Highway until she saw a help wanted sign in a small, grubby pizza place in Freeport Plaza, beneath the elevated Long Island Railroad tracks. A crooked blue sign flashed above scratched glass doors. The place was permeated with the odor of garlic and sweat, seeping onto the street.

She paused and looked in the window. It was called the *Pizza Baas*. She knew the dive – kids went there to get cheap eats. It languished in the shadows.

Moeda would hate it.

Ayla went inside, and stepped up to the counter.

"I want to apply for a job."

Sal, the owner, was at the cash register. He eyed her up and down, pausing at her breasts.

"It doesn't look like you need a job."

"I don't care how it looks, I want a job."

He nodded. "I'm Sal – I own the place. It's a classy pizza restaurant."

Ayla looked around. There wasn't anything classy about the place except for the few tables with red-checked tablecloths.

"It's called the Pizza Baas because my wife insisted on a Dutch name," Sal continued, boasting. "She's a descendant of New Amsterdam shopkeepers. *Baas* meant boss, and I'm the boss of the Freeport Train Station.

Ayla tried not to laugh.

"I always try to make a woman happy," Sal added, licking his lips.

"That's the most important thing," she mumbled.

"How old are you?" Sal asked.

"Old enough."

"OK, you got the job. Off the books, no working papers."

Ayla nodded. "When do I start?"

"Tomorrow. After school. "I'll train you myself."

Ayla wondered what kind of training it took to work in a pizza dive, but she kept quiet. She stared at Sal's fat, soft fingers. They were twitching. Ayla couldn't wait to get home and tell Moeda.

It was exactly as Ayla expected.

Moeda hated Pizza Baas and begged Ayla to work in a better neighborhood.

"Can't you find a job in Meroke or Smithville?" Moeda begged to no avail. "They're so much . . . nicer."

"I want to work in the real world," Ayla smirked, "not in a copy of old Hollywood."

11

Her life changed with the job.

Kids loved Pizza Baas, along with the illegals who wore sagging blue jeans and worn tee shirts; laborers looking for cheap eats; and families who wanted a quick fix, avoiding pricier places like *Outback* in Meroke and *Applebee's* in Smithville. During rush hours, commuters often stopped by, hungry for a quick slice before facing tumultuous homes. Most people from Meroke avoided the place, picturing roaches and mice in the storeroom. It was weird that an upscale rich kid from The Gables would work at a place like Pizza Baas.

Ayla loved the rep. She was hired because Sal thought she was hot. It wasn't legal without working papers but no one asked. Sal paid her cash in crumpled, sticky bills. Sometimes Ayla wondered why the bills were so sticky. The thought of an old guy jerking off into piles of pizza and dollars made her laugh until tears ran down her face.

Men couldn't keep their eyes off Ayla. She'd smile and old guys stared, licking their lips. She'd shake her hips and dudes wiggled in their pants. Ayla's sultry glances, deep voice, and teasing smile taunted them. At the same time, she squared her narrow shoulders, held her head high, and moved with an aristocratic gait that screamed she belonged somewhere else. Sal loved it – he displayed his girl like a diamond in a foxhole. Sal, soft and middle-aged with thick fat fingers, made sure he patted her every time she did something right. His fingers wandered over her expensive clothes, drifting into dangerous places. Ayla didn't mind. She never stopped him; she would shift her position, give him a quick feel, and edge away pretending she had no clue what happened.

It drove Sal crazy.

Pizza Baas food was made from the cheapest ingredients Sal could buy. The crust was thick and chewy, the cheese melted in gooey clumps, and the tomato sauce came from dented cans stored on a shelf black with mouse droppings. Sometimes Sal would sprinkle bits of waxy pepperoni, extra cheese, or sliced onions to make "specialty pies" so he could rig up the price. The final topping was always thin, watery green oil dribbled over each pie, leaving a Rorschach blotch of grease on the paper plates.

It was a different world from the sushi and lobster salads Ayla shared with Moeda, or the glittering technology that populated their home. Sometimes Ayla nibbled at a slice until the oil dribbled down her chin. Sal followed its path into the cleavage between her breasts. His eyes bulged. She laughed inside and wiggled like an upscale stripper.

It made her feel sexy – like an actress in a porn flick. She played with Sal like she once played with the expensive toys Moeda brought home. They were all designed to fill the gaping hole inside – the part of Ayla left raw and unclaimed.

Ayla worked at Pizza Baas every day after school. She hated school, couldn't tolerate adolescent chatter, and was bored by her entitled classmates. She had no friends and liked it that way. Her grades were good so the school left her alone. Ayla had always been a loner, never part of the neighborhood buzz – an outlier in her world.

No one cared. No one talked to her and no one asked for anything. When she was bored, Ayla hooked up with one of the high school boys and disappeared into the back seat of a BMW or the hidden corner of a darkened home theater for quick, numbing sex.

Ayla didn't care anymore. She would never forgive Moeda for her lies.

12

Three weeks later, on a grey afternoon, Ayla looked through the Pizza Baas window.

A gang roared down Sunrise Highway, electrifying the wide, bland roadway. It seethed with danger. People watched in awe. They whispered that the only way someone became a member was to commit murder. It didn't matter *who* they killed – just that they took another life.

The gang traveled in a blur of black, silver, and bike fumes. On the street, everyone moved out of their way. Ayla's heart raced.

Daddy would hate them.

The gang stopped in front of the Pizza Baas and surveyed the area. Locals were afraid of the skinheads and white supremacists on bikes, flaunting their politics from tee shirts, patches, and tattoos. Teens and wannabes avoided them, bystanders lowered their eyes and scurried away from the grizzled faces. They meant blood. Black and Latino shopkeepers were anxious, gays stayed away, and Jews locked their homes and synagogues.

Ayla was awed. They took her breath away. Big and powerful, the bikers defied everyone. They weren't afraid. They ruled wherever they went as if emerging from a movie screen that no one could shut down.

Mack was the oldest – their leader. Some said he was 50, others whispered that he was 52. Ayla was never sure and wouldn't dare ask.

They stomped into Pizza Baas, changing the space into a sea of sleeveless black leather jackets, tee shirts, tattoos, and swaggering arrogance. Customers left quietly, emptying the few available chairs and tables. The bikers said nothing, watching the fleeing diners as if they were rodents scurrying for safety.

Ayla was mesmerized. Mack pushed his way through the men. It wasn't hard – they stepped aside obediently like the Red Sea parting for Moses. Mack grinned. He was a man who knew his power.

"I want pizza," he snarled.

Ayla stared at him.

"Bitch."

The bikers laughed.

"Don't call me bitch," Ayla said softly. She was terrified but refused to let him see her fear.

"You are a bitch."

She shook her head. "I'm Ayla."

Mack eyed her for a long time. There was dead silence in Pizza Baas. The bikers tensed for a fight. No one back-talked Mack – not even a classy white girl.

"How old are you, bitch?"

"Sixteen," Ayla raised her chin defiantly.

"Jailbait," someone taunted.

Mack laughed. "I like jailbait. Young meat is fucking sweet."

The guys roared, licked their lips, and rubbed their crotches. Ayla had never seen the dance live. She was alarmed and intrigued at the same time.

Mack leaned over the counter. The tip of his tongue curled across his bottom lip. His dark eyes gleamed with raw sexuality. Ayla held her breath. Mack reached out and grabbed her hair. His fingers were filled with promise. Ayla froze. Suddenly the fingers changed. She wondered how such an old guy could be so fierce and still have a gentle touch.

"Ayla," he hissed. "Bitch. You're mine."

It sounded like the lyrics in a rap.

Mack ran his fingers down her neck and across her shoulder. He paused, inches from her breast. Ayla couldn't breathe.

He wasn't like Sal groping for a quick feel. He wasn't like the high school boys grabbing and spurting. Mack had promise – his fingers taunted her, his eyes broadcast temptation that she was unable to resist. He made her feel alluring – sexy inside and out.

Gently, Mack ran the tip of his index finger over her breast. Ayla watched, unable to move.

"Pizza," he growled. "Now. For all of us."

Ayla stared at his fingers and then into his eyes.

He had her.

"Now," she whispered. She didn't notice the groans of approval, like the cheers of a fundraising crowd, behind Mack.

Hands trembling, Ayla put an entire pie in front of him. The ceiling lights reflected off of one edge, as if warning her that something very hot was about to happen.

Ayla ignored it.

Mack pulled out a single slice and licked the cheese, his tongue slowly demonstrating his prowess.

"You'll get your turn Ayla," he cooed, then snapped off the tip with his teeth.

Ayla jumped.

"More," Mack ordered and turned away. "For these hungry men."

As the gang swarmed the counter, Ayla realized she had never asked Mack to pay.

13

Mack and his gang finally left.

"I'll be back," he growled.

Sal heard everything. He waited until the shop was empty except for a single, pimply kid at the cash register. He waved Ayla into the storeroom and closed the door behind them.

"You like the biker guy?" He asked hoarsely.

"Yeah." Ayla watched him breathing hard.

"He says you're a bitch and belong to him."

Ayla tossed her hair, not responding.

"Well," Sal hitched up his pants, "he's wrong."

"Why?"

"You belong to me."

Ayla laughed.

Sal didn't smile. "You know what that means . . . bitch?"

She shrugged.

"If you want to keep your job – see your biker friend again – you have to take care of me."

Sal's hands quivered and trickles of sweat dribbled down his face.

"What do you want?"

"This." He dropped his pants and showed his erection. Ayla stared. "You must be kidding."

"No," he grabbed her arm. "Do me."

"I keep my job?"

"Yeah, as long as you do me."

"You give me a raise? And all the pizza I want."

"Yeah."

She thought of Moeda and The Senator. She could play like them – sex for food and money.

"Sure," Ayla fell to her knees and took the panting man into her mouth. "Deal."

14

While Sal recovered in the storeroom, Ayla went back to the front window. She stared at the dust left by the bikers. Ayla was drawn to the angry men who rode black *Harleys* and terrified people wherever they went. She longed to be one of them.

She went shopping that week by herself, using Moeda's credit card. She bought tight, low-slung frayed jeans and a rhinestone-and-black leather belt, along with shiny leather boots with four-inch spiked heels that rose to her knees. She purchased a snug black tee that left a swath of skin along her middle, revealing her new silver belly button ring.

The kids at school called her a biker chick.

She laughed.

Ayla waited for the gang to return.

She dreamed about the bikers – reckless and mean; loners like herself; confronting the world, one-by-one; against traffic.

Ayla knew they would come back for her.

15

Mack returned at the perfect time.

The day was bathed in grey. The wind howled like feral cats and rain threatened, but refused to let loose as if set in pause.

"Now," Mack ordered her.

Ayla left work and they silently walked to his apartment. She never questioned him.

The place was off Sunrise Highway, behind a factory, and below a house filled with druggies who sold and used everything from heroin to meth. Ayla loved it. The house had a buzz – exciting, dangerous, and on the edge of evil.

Ayla looked at the water tower before she entered the apartment, as if asking for permission.

The tower had seen it all. Freeport had a water tower – or pumping station – since the 1890s. It was a town accustomed to controversy. In 1924, 30,000 spectators lined the street to watch a procession of thousands of robed Ku Klux Klan members, led by the Village Police Chief. During the Prohibition era, Freeport Point Shipyard built boats for rumrunners. Freeport evolved into a diverse community with poorer minorities living in buildings and small homes, wealthier families in the south near the water, and mostly illegal day laborers looking for work.

Freeport was very different from Ayla's Hollywood wannabe home in The Gables.

Mack opened the door. "It's time," he said, not looking at her. "Time for me to own you."

Inside, it was dark, damp, and smelled of mildew. Ayla was excited by the intrigue, entering the domain of the devil.

Mack led her to a bare mattress in the shadowy area designated as a bedroom. A partial wall separated the mattress from the rest of the space. Ayla had only seen places like this on the screen – gloomy, decrepit, and treacherous. Her heart pounded as she waited for his next move.

Mack stared at her for what felt like forever. He peeled off her clothes, touching her skin where he bared it. She didn't move. He dropped her clothes on the floor. She wanted him to strip but Mack did nothing. After several torturous minutes, Ayla fell to her knees and unzipped his jeans. Mack was silent. She pulled down his pants and took him into her mouth. Mack groaned as she worked him. He put his hands on her hair and pressed her face harder against him. Unlike her teenage lovers, he held back, rigid with pleasure.

Suddenly he pulled her off of him. Ayla held her breath.

Mack smiled crookedly and yanked off his clothes. Ayla watched, mesmerized by his tattoos; aroused by the Nazi Iron Eagle on his chest. He fell to his knees and pushed her onto the mattress.

"Bitch," he muttered.

Ayla cried as he leaped on top of her and savagely bit her nipples.

Sex was different with him. While he wasn't as big and hard as her classmate lovers, he was slow and delicious, lasting forever. He brought her to a frenzy that she never imagined could exist; she lost herself in the wild, uncontained assault on her body. She was electrified as if a switch had been turned on, and she was thrust into a breathless sensual descent. His tongue traced every inch of her skin; his fingers left nothing untouched, probing into every crevice, every fold, until she was burning, grabbing at him, begging him to finish her. Yet he took longer, making her dance in his power, forcing climaxes that left her weak and giddy.

"I own you," he said thickly.

Finally, in an explosive roar like a Harley on open road, he plunged into her and finished.

It took a long time to recover. Slowly, Ayla caught her breath and opened her eyes. She stared at him like a little kid dancing in a horror flick.

Mack laughed. "You can fuck your pimply schoolmates but there's nothing like an old man who knows where to put it."

Ayla didn't understand what he meant. It didn't matter. As she traced the gritty lines of the Nazi Iron Eagle tattoo on his chest, she knew one thing.

I'm his.

16

Time performed its lethal dance.

Ayla fell in love with Mack *and* his basement apartment although it was not much more than a windowless hole. It was furnished with a stained mattress and splintery fruit crates for tables and chairs. Mack found an ancient cooler in the trash, regularly filled it with ice, and transformed it into his "refrigerator." Someone gave him a hotplate if he wanted to plug into the single outlet to cook. The toilet was old and rusted, screeching unhappily when flushed; the shower was a corner with a head and no curtain. Everything was covered in a film of oily dirt as if plucked from an ancient lair.

Upstairs, the druggies did a brisk business. Ayla forced herself not to listen to the eerie silences, inhuman grunts, or beatings that pierced the music. She took possession of her space and Mack, accepting both without question.

At home, Moeda was frozen into silence. Her world was transformed into a scenario she didn't recognize. Ayla constructed a wall, thick and impenetrable, like her biological father. Moeda tried to talk but Ayla turned her back. Moeda suggested dinners and shopping trips but Ayla refused.

Mack is my life now.

Days and weeks passed. Ayla started cutting classes and going late to Pizza Baas. Sal grumbled but Ayla didn't care. As long as she took care of him in the storeroom, Sal let everything pass.

Ayla was in a movie-without-end; a bizarre screenplay that kept her breathless each day, not knowing what Mack would do or say, not knowing whether Mack would be angry or loving, not knowing anything but the heart-pounding thrill of *now*. She counted the minutes until they were immersed in sex where each moment brought a new experience, a new way to enhance their passion. Ayla learned more about herself in a few hours with Mack than she had in all of her 16 years.

Mack taught her how to steal money from Pizza Baas; Sal didn't dare confront her. He wasn't going to take on Mack and his bikers or risk losing his interludes in the storeroom. Ayla smiled coyly and allowed him to grab at her breasts as she sucked him.

She used the extra cash to buy beer for Mack.

Ayla couldn't get enough of Mack. If they weren't making love, she just watched him, awed by his muscles and pulsating tattoos. She loved to hear him bark commands at the guys and loved it more when they obeyed. She knew the bikers were doing some really bad stuff – breaking into houses, selling drugs, and stealing money. It didn't matter. All she wanted was to belong to Mack.

Once, Ayla told Mack about The Senator.

Mack laughed. "Sure. "Everyone has a famous father."

Ayla shut up. She wasn't surprised that Mack didn't believe her. Why should he? She also wasn't surprised when the shoves and fists came. Wasn't that what they showed in the movies? Ayla knew it was always her fault. She put him in a bad mood. She chose the wrong words. She pretended the spankings and rough sex was play. Mack knew everything. It was Ayla's fault when Mack lost his temper – she had to work harder to keep him happy.

Mack increased his demands.

"I want you here whenever I need you," he growled one day when Ayla returned from school. "A man needs his bitch."

Ayla shivered.

Mack pushed her against the rough concrete wall. He roared in her ear. "You're mine bitch. You do what I want."

Ayla's heart raced as he ripped off her clothes. He plunged into her without foreplay. It hurt.

Ayla was dizzy – strangely, she liked it when it hurt – it made her feel alive and totally possessed by his power.

When he finished, Ayla collapsed on the floor. Mack loomed overhead, studying her face. Ayla smiled sweetly.

"Cunt," he snarled and kicked her in the ribs with the steel toe of his Dr. Marten boot. "It's time to teach you a *real* lesson."

She howled. "Why?"

Mack laughed. "A bitch has to learn."

He kicked her again. Then he used his fists – on her face, breasts and belly. Finally, he turned and left her on the floor. Ayla heard his Harley rev up and everything went black.

Ayla laid there for hours. The cold damp eventually woke her. She was naked, her body covered in bruises. Her ribs hurt

– something was probably broken. Carefully, she dressed herself in the ripped clothes and made her way back to Moeda.

17

Everything looked different. Home was no longer safe; her street strange and unwelcoming.

What's happening?

Ayla opened the front door and shouted hello. Her voice, weak from the beating, sounded old and craggy, like the homes in The Gables.

Moeda's mouth dropped when she saw Ayla. "My God, what happened to you?"

"Calm down. It's no big deal."

Moeda's eyes bulged. "*No big deal?*" she shrieked. "Look at you."

"Fuck you," Ayla snapped.

They faced off.

Moeda took a deep breath. Her eyes narrowed and her mouth became a straight, hard line. "What's going on?" She asked through clenched teeth.

"Nothing."

"You're sleeping with him."

"So?"

"I shouldn't have told you about your father."

Ayla shrugged.

"It was my choice," Moeda lowered her eyes. She rubbed her hands together. "All my choice."

For a moment, Ayla felt sorry for Moeda. She imagined her at 16, bright-eyed and optimistic, winning the political internship that guaranteed a future. She saw Moeda happy, eager to please.

Then she saw her father. Unzipping his pants and drawing the teenager into his hideous embrace.

"I thought I loved him," Moeda whispered.

"He was 26 years older than you."

"That's what made him so appealing. He was older and important . . . and he wanted *me*. You understand. I know you understand about . . . older men."

Moeda's eyes went dark. She knows, Ayla thought, but she doesn't realize that Mack is nothing like The Senator.

"Leave me alone," Ayla snapped. "Just leave me alone."

"Wait," Moeda cried pitifully. It was too late. Sixteen years too late.

"I'm done waiting, Moeda. I'm done with you, the checks, and this fucking Hollywood rip-off."

"You can't be done. You're too young."

"Try me. I hate you and The Senator and everything you stand for."

"You hate yourself," Moeda said softly. "I know what *that* feels like."

Ayla shrugged.

"He beat you, Ayla. Don't you see? It's not about you – it's about him."

"So? He loves me. He's going to take care of me, not like you."

"He's going to fuck you until he's bored," she snarled.

"You have no idea," Ayla screamed. "What do you know about love . . . men? What do you care? The only thing you care about are those stupid souvenirs that you sell to tourists who think they're getting a real piece of Long Island. Well look around, Moeda, this is the real deal and it's not pretty. Mack doesn't have to do anything because I *want* to fuck him. I like it. It makes me feel good . . ."

Moeda dropped her voice to a whisper. "He hurts you."

"I deserve it."

Their eyes locked.

"Don't do this," Moeda begged. "You'll regret it for the rest of your life."

"Like you regret me?"

"I didn't say that."

Ayla sniffed. "You didn't have to . . ."

"Please . . ."

"I'm moving in with him. Permanently."

She turned and left, headed back to Mack. She had a place to go and a man who wanted her. When she arrived at the basement apartment, Mack wasn't home.

Ayla ripped off her clothes, flung herself across the mattress, and fell asleep, dreaming about Nazi Iron Eagles and political fundraisers.

18

Ayla woke the next morning to Mack looming above her.

"Get up," he ordered.

She sat up, trembling. He stared at her. "Get dressed."

Ayla didn't question him. She dressed quickly.

"We're going out."

He led her into the sunlight. They strapped on helmets, climbed aboard the Harley, and roared through the suburban streets. He headed for the Throgs Neck Bridge, weaving through a chorus of honks, trucks, and cursing drivers. Mack was oblivious. She had no idea where he was taking her. They raced across the bridge and on the Cross Bronx Expressway. He bypassed the George Washington Bridge, heading upstate to the Tappan Zee to cross the Hudson River.

Even when they hit Palisades Interstate Parkway, Ayla was clueless. She only knew they were leaving Long Island behind them.

Mack raced the bike for over two hours, going too fast, cutting off cars, and nearly colliding with trucks. He chose an exit Ayla didn't recognize and followed a two-lane road that snaked into the mountains.

Ayla saw a small sign. *Bear Mountain State Park.*

They entered a different world. There were no voices, trucks, buses, and sirens. The air was filled with the whoosh of leaves, birdsong, and the soft scatter of tiny animals. Everything smelled different. Ayla sucked in deep breaths, savoring the fragrance of the country. She loved the wind in her hair, the bike between her legs, Mack's body pressed close, and the freedom of no one else.

The two of them, like a God and His Follower, blasted into a world where only select people were invited. Ayla pushed the beating from her mind. It was her initiation into his world and she had passed. She was one of *them.*

Mack slowed the bike and cut into a narrow, bumpy road that ended on a dirt path.

Where are we going? Was there more to the initiation?

The trail was choked with trees; Mack had to steer carefully to avoid being caught by low hanging branches. The trees finally thinned into a tiny clearing. Mack stopped, climbed off the bike and removed his helmet. He gently removed her helmet and placed them both on the seat. He took her hand and led her to the edge.

They stood on a cliff that overlooked the Hudson River. Mack squeezed her hand, sharing the breath taking view of old, rounded mountains and deep valleys. The trees were thick with occasional spots of bare rock. Far below them was the Hudson, flowing like a blue glass ribbon reflecting sky and clouds. Higher peaks covered with trees and topped with low-lying white clouds shimmered in the distance.

It was the most beautiful place she'd ever seen.

Mack dropped her hand and returned to the bike. Ayla couldn't take her eyes from the view. It was as if she were suddenly plunged into timelessness where nothing and no one could touch her. She heard Mack busy with something. Ayla didn't want to turn around; didn't want to take her eyes from the world beneath her feet.

If he's going to kill me here, it's okay. Just one push.

"Ayla," Mack said softly.

She turned.

Mack had taken a red-checked tablecloth from Pizza Baas and spread it on the ground. He unscrewed a bottle of cheap wine and balanced two paper cups against it. There was a pile of paper napkins and a cardboard bucket with fried chicken.

Ayla stared at the picnic.

"Look," Mack held up a chocolate-covered strawberry. "I thought you would like this."

Ayla was mesmerized by the delicate strawberry dangling between his rough, road-blackened fingers.

"Take it." Mack grinned boyishly.

Cautiously, Ayla reached for the strawberry. Mack nodded. Suddenly he grabbed her and dragged her to the edge. She didn't know whether to fight him or do nothing.

"In your mouth," Mack ordered.

Ayla put the strawberry between her lips.

"Do you trust me?"

She nodded.

He held her at the edge of the cliff. "Let's see how much."

Mack grabbed Ayla under her armpits and lifted her off her feet. He dangled her over the edge. It was a drop of hundreds of feet of exposed rocks, jagged trees, and razor-sharp edges, to the river. She opened her mouth to scream and the chocolate-covered strawberry fell, bouncing off the rocks below. It splattered before hitting the river.

"Silence," Mack roared.

Ayla trembled but didn't scream.

"I own you," he said evenly. "You're my sex slave. Hear? *My sex slave.* You're my property. I can do whatever I want with you."

Her eyes were locked on the fall. How long would it take to die if Mack chose to drop her?

"Answer me." He smiled, smelling her terror.

"Y . . . yes." She managed.

"The only thing between your life and death is me. Do you understand?"

He loosened his grip as if he would release her. "Do you understand?"

She closed her eyes.

"Look at me."

She obeyed.

"I own you," Mack said pleasantly. "I can drop you whenever I want, get back on my bike, leave, and no one would find you for a long time. You'll be a shattered, bloody body in the river. Maybe the water will take you downstream into the city and New York Harbor. You can rot next to the Statue of Liberty." He laughed, loosening his grip. "Maybe not. Maybe the animals will get you first for dinner." He grinned. "Do you get it Ayla? Do you really get it?"

"Y . . . yes."

He nodded and tightened his grip.

"Please . . ."

"Please what, bitch?"

"Don't kill me."

"That's not good enough."

"Take me," Ayla choked. "Please take me."

"Ahhhhh," Mack said sweetly. "Almost there."

Ayla was so terrified, she could hardly speak, but she knew the words. "You own me," she choked. "My life is in your hands. I'm your sex slave."

Mack grinned.

He pulled her back from the edge and settled her on solid ground. Tears ran down her face as he pressed her against him, his erection as hard as the rocks below.

She trembled violently. Sweat covered her body. He thrust his hand between her legs. "I see you like this as much as me, bitch."

Ayla was terrified.

And crazy excited.

19

He led her to the red-checked tablecloth on the ground.

"Sit."

Ayla sat.

Mack towered over her. Slowly, he sat, never taking his eyes from her face. He crossed his legs and took her hand. "This is a . . . special place," he said tonelessly.

Ayla nodded.

"I've never taken anyone here," he lied, his eyes scanning the scene. "You're the first."

Ayla believed him.

"There's another side of me . . ." he paused. "I keep it tight. You know. I don't want people to think I'm weak. That's why . . . well, I had to show you who's in control. I let you live. Or die. Only me. Do you get that?"

She looked at his big, coarse hand gripping hers. Mack waited as she returned her gaze to his face. "I get it," she said hoarsely.

He dropped her hand and ran his calloused fingertips gently down her cheek, tracing the bruises he had left.

"My momma – the fucking drunk – always told me to remember that strong trees grow tender buds. Know what I mean? I'm the strongest man you'll ever know. If you behave, I'm also tender. Do you know what I want now?"

Ayla got it. She leaned over and kissed him.

Mack grinned. "Sometimes I get angry. Sometimes I get mean. Sometimes I'm going to hurt you. I want you to know that."

"I know that."

"I like to kill," he grabbed both of her hands and squeezed until they hurt. "I like the smell of blood. Understand?"

Suddenly Ayla plunged into a dream. *Beauty and The Beast.* She saw the beloved, independent Belle with the hideous beast who had the soul of a prince. The Beast imprisoned Belle. If he wanted to return to his human form, he had to earn Belle's love or remain a beast forever. It was a daunting task.

Ayla knew exactly what she had to do.

I'll find the prince in Mack.

The beast will be gone.

"I understand," Ayla whispered.

Mack opened his arms to embrace the scenery and her acceptance. In that moment they were seamless; characters in a story that cried to be told.

"Beautiful," Mack mumbled.

"I love you," Ayla said with the full force of her 16 years.

Mack made a soft, growling noise.

"I love you," Ayla said again.

"Thank you," Mack said finally. He pushed her flat on the blanket and made love gently as if she was a porcelain doll and he was afraid to break her.

He never said "I love you."

20

Ayla skipped the next four days of school, sleeping in Mack's place. Each day she savored the time spent with him, recalling the dizzying view of his gentler side along with the terror of his power when he dangled her over the cliff. It brought an edge to their relationship; an enigma she could treasure. Mack belonged to Ayla, although he didn't realize it, as much as she belonged to him. Ayla expanded the moment into a romantic epiphany. She was the owner of a grown man scarred by life; the possessor of his hidden heart; the holder of his soul. She controlled the murderer.

It progressed like a tacky romance novel.

The days passed and Ayla made sure she was in the apartment when Mack left for 'work' and returned for sex. He brought her pink-frosted cupcakes, chocolate chip cookies, and said the right things. She forgot about the anger and the bruises; ignored the terror of being dangled over the cliff; looked past his flat eyes that only softened when he talked about power and murder.

Ayla shifted from The Senator to her new love. Mack was beautiful inside and exciting outside.

"If you behave," Mack reminded her, "you get good things – good things for good cunts."

Ayla hung on his words, eager to please him. She worked harder to do anything he wanted – anything he asked – whether or not she liked it.

"You got it bitch," he said affectionately. "Piss me off and things won't work. I own you, don't forget that."

She texted Moeda.

> I'm ok. I'm not coming home again. I'm 16 and it's my right. Call the police and I'll go public and u will lose your checks. Everyone will know about my father. B smart. U dont want Mack and his gang coming after you. They love to kill.

> Did I tell you about Mack's favorite hunter combat knife?

Ayla added an image of the combat knife to the text.

Ayla knew Moeda was terrified. She could see her mother sitting on the couch beneath the cornfields swaying in oiled winds, eyes red, staring into space, wine glass in hand, and waiting.

Waiting.

She deserved it, Ayla thought, for trading my birth right for a check and a Hollywood wannabe house. Moeda was as despicable as The Senator. Ayla hated them both.

"I want you here waiting for me," Mack demanded. "All the time. I want you ready."

"You want me to quit Pizza Baas?"

"No. I like the food and the money. I can always use extra money. It's school. Fuck school. You're old enough to ditch the place."

Ayla had never considered that.

"Yeah," Mack repeated. "That's what I want – you have to quit school and make me happy. Quit the fucking school."

Ayla saw herself on TV at a fancy fundraiser. Daddy was shaking the President's hand. They were surrounded by their families. Patriotic music roared in the background and red-white-and-blue balloons filled the air. Moeda sat wide-eyed in the audience.

Suddenly Ayla entered the picture with her biker clothes and Mack. She wore a black leather jacket with a large Nazi Iron Eagle patch.

Hello Senator. I'm your daughter the dropout.

Ayla laughed. "Sure Mack, anything you want. What does it matter? I'll still work at Pizza Baas."

"Good. Free money and food. I'll take it."

Ayla giggled and told him what she did to Sal in the storeroom. Mack was silent. They never spoke about it again.

The next day she went to school and quit.

Ayla was officially done.

21

She didn't know exactly when it began.

Ayla's periods stopped and her belly swelled. She felt different – bigger and fuller. There were odd cravings, like the cheap pepperoni Sal used on his pizzas, and peanut-butter filled pretzels from *Trader Joe's*. She ate more than usual but hid it from Mack, buying and eating cheap junk food outside the apartment. Ayla checked some of the symptoms online and although she didn't want to accept what was happening, she *knew*.

Ayla didn't tell Mack anything.

She spent more time at Pizza Baas, stole more money from the cash register, and dined on paper plates filled with pepperoni slices. Now that she quit school and didn't live with Moeda, there was nothing to keep her from working more hours.

Sal's demands increased. Some days, she spent more time in the storeroom than behind the counter. Instead of being satisfied, Sal became greedier, wanting her more often. She refused to have sex with him, but allowed him to fondle her breasts and finger her as she worked on his penis. Inside, Ayla laughed. Sal was pitiful next to Mack. His penis was small, his body fleshy and soft, his groans subdued so no one would hear.

Everyone heard him. They laughed and taunted Ayla but she didn't care. As Mack's girlfriend she could get any one of them killed if she wanted - or beaten up, with broken legs and lots of blood. It made *her* laugh. She, like Mack, felt God-like. Sal amused her so she let it continue, the storeroom providing a different kind of adventure in her new life.

Fat, pitiful Sal loved her.

Ayla ate more pizza, happy with her life for the first time she could remember. She would stare at the lumpy cheese and grease stains on her slice and wonder if it was like tea leaves, concealing a message or a fortune. She wanted to know more about this baby growing inside her, but the pizza told her nothing.

Sometimes, Mack would make sex demands that were uglier than Sal's. It was always the same scenario. He would bring some gang members into his apartment who he wanted to "reward." He would announce that she was his "sex slave" and do anything they wanted.

If she objected, Mack would beat her.

Ayla obeyed.

"Do any sex thing you want," Mack instructed his men, "but don't fuck her. That's for me and me alone."

Usually there were only one or two guys in the apartment, waiting their turn. Sometimes there were as many as six. Ayla never knew when or who to expect.

Mack loved to watch. After the guys were gone, Mack would make love to her gently. Ayla loved those times.

That's how she knew Mack loved her more than pathetic Sal.

22

The first months of pregnancy were idyllic. Ayla felt the baby growing inside and revelled in the flutters that were the first movements. She blossomed with her secret, convinced that Mack would never refuse his child. Then Ayla would show her father and the world that she could do whatever she wanted. What a twist for the Man with Power and Money and a biker son-in-law. Everything was perfect.

Until Mack noticed.

She caught him staring at her belly when she was sprawled naked on the mattress after sex.

"You got yourself knocked up," Mack said in a flat voice.

"It's yours, Mack. There's no one else."

"The bitch got herself knocked up," Mack repeated, a fire igniting his eyes.

Ayla knew the signs. "It's yours, Mack," she said again, cowering.

Mack stood up from the mattress and towered over her. He kicked her in the belly. Rage smoldered, and then exploded. He kicked her over and over, in the belly, groin, breasts, and back. Ayla rolled into a fetal position trying to ward off the blows. Mack fell to his knees and beat her with his fists, breaking her nose, swelling her eyes, and leaving angry bruises in his wake. He leaped up and dragged her across the floor, skinning her back and legs.

Then he raped her.

When Mack was finished he stared at his work. Ayla couldn't move. Mack shook his head.

"You shouldn't have done this," he growled. "It's all your fault."

She wanted to tell him that it was all about *love*; he didn't need to beat her. There was a life they could both own; a *thing* that a part of them. *Beauty and The Beast,* she thought.

Ayla couldn't speak.

Mack paced in front of her, his anger satiated.

"I should kill you," he snarled. "Kill you, make you bleed out, get rid of the fucker inside you. Yeah, that's what I should do. Give you a taste of my hunter combat knife. Maybe I should have the guys rape you first . . . torture you like they love to do and . . ."

He glanced at her.

"I can't," he mumbled.

Mack grabbed his stuff and left. Ayla could barely see him through her swollen eyes but she heard the unmistakable roar of his Harley.

She was alone. Her fantasy of Ayla, Mack and the baby was shattered. She crawled into a corner and hid.

Mack was gone for almost two weeks.

She nursed herself during that time, never venturing out from the basement. She called in sick at Pizza Baas. Sal tried to reach her but she ignored him. Moeda left texts and voice mails but Ayla refused to reply. One day Moeda knocked on the door and Ayla told her to go away.

"Please come home," Moeda begged. "I don't care what you've done. We'll figure it out. Just get away from this monster."

Ayla didn't answer. How did her mother *know*?

Hours later, when Ayla peered through the door, she saw that Moeda left two bags of groceries.

Ayla texted Moeda.

Dont ever come back.

Ayla's bruises turned from red to purple and began to disappear. The swelling went down and she could see again. The bleeding stopped although her nose would remain crooked for the rest of her life. Ayla stayed alone, living on Moeda's groceries, and waiting for Mack to come home.

One night she heard a kitten mewing at the door. Ayla opened it a crack and saw the tiny creature, most probably abandoned by her mother. Ayla took the kitten inside and shared her food with the animal. In return, the kitten crawled into her lap, purring loudly. It was oddly comforting.

Ayla gave the kitten a name. Cat.

Cat watched each morning as Ayla awoke on the mattress and pounded her swollen belly. Something had changed. The baby she once loved was now her victim.

"I hate you, I hate you," she screamed at the growing fetus.

Each day when there was no blood to show that she miscarried, Ayla shouted through her tears.

"Die! Die!"

The baby held on. Neither Ayla nor Mack could deny their child life.

Cat crawled into her lap and purred, comforting Ayla.

When Ayla finally heard Mack's Harley pull into the driveway, she grabbed Cat and threw the animal out the door. Ayla didn't want another dead kitten.

Mack entered the apartment. He sniffed the air as if he sensed there was a cat around. Ayla had been careful – she left no traces.

Mack tossed a worn straw picnic basket on the floor.

He looked old and tired. Some of the fire had bled from his eyes. He sat on a fruit carton.

Ayla shied away, hitching her knees as high as her belly would permit.

"I'm not going to kill you," Mack said, his voice oddly resigned. "I thought about that for a while but it won't work." He took a deep breath. "It's not that I haven't killed people before but this time . . ." He paused. "I have brats all over, you know. Every time one of my bitches got herself knocked up, I skipped out. I wanted no part of that scene. It's not me."

Mack ran his fingers through his grey hair. "I never knew any of the kids and that was good. Very good."

Ayla held her breath.

"One bitch threatened to call the cops on me for child support. I told her to go ahead. I didn't care. One night I would creep into her house and kill her, the kid, and her mother. No one would ever know who did it."

"What happened?" Ayla whispered.

"I never heard from her again." he laughed, baring tobacco-stained teeth.

Ayla thought of Moeda.

"You're right," he read her thoughts. "I'd kill *your* mother, too."

Ayla gasped.

Mack rubbed his jaw. "Here's the deal. I want to keep you around." He looked at her belly. "It's too late to beat the kid out of you. So have it. Right here," he tilted his head toward the mattress. "If it's kicking, I'll take it to the cops."

Mack reached into his pocket and handed her a crumpled brochure. Ayla's hands trembled, as she read the words.

You've hidden your pregnancy . . .
You couldn't let anyone know . . .
Don't panic.
There's a SECRET SAFE PLACE for newborns.

State law allows a mother who believes she cannot care for her baby to legally and safely leave the newborn at a number of locations, including police precincts, firehouses, hospitals, churches or with any responsible adult willing to accept the baby and call proper authorities. It's a Safe Haven for you and your child.

It was the same as the sign she saw on Merrick Road.

Mack waited for her to finish reading.

"I checked out a cop station in Seaford. Far enough away from us. They have one of those signs in front: *Safe Babies – Safe Place – Safe Haven.* We can leave the kid and no one will know who we are. Then you, me and the guys will split. We'll go far away from here – due west. I never want to talk about this. I'll get you some pills so it doesn't happen again."

A thick lump formed in her throat. Ayla wanted to scream – to hold onto this thing in her belly.

Mack was giving her a choice.

Like Moeda and The Senator.

"If you don't . . . I'll take my hunter combat knife to the kid. Slice it up. Then on to you . . ." He paused. "By the looks of it, we don't have a long time to wait."

Ayla wanted desperately to ask him the question.

Don't you want it?

Don't you want your baby?

Moeda had asked the same question – the answers led to a lifetime of lies. How many times did Moeda see The Senator on TV, read about him in the newspaper, or watch him online?

Ayla couldn't live Moeda's life. She couldn't sacrifice everything for a baby.

"You still want me?"

"That's the only way. We get rid of it and never turn back – never talk about it, never tell anyone. Done."

She looked at the brochure. Safe Haven. It was Mack or the baby. Ayla made her decision.

I won't follow in Moeda's footsteps.

"Done," Ayla said firmly.

Mack nodded. He grabbed a can of beer from the cooler and drank to their decision.

Done deal.

23

Ayla nuzzled the baby. He was so tiny. Ayla didn't know exact dates so she couldn't figure out if he was born early. She had never seen a doctor about being pregnant; never took prenatal vitamins or asked questions. She had been too busy pretending it would go away.

Ayla took a deep breath. Now that the baby was in her arms, things changed. She wondered why he cried so hard at first and then didn't cry at all. Why was he so sleepy? Maybe she should have called before labor began? Maybe the voice would have told her what to do?

It was too late. After all that happened, after Moeda and her lies, Sal and his storeroom, Mack and his fists, too many decisions were made. There was no turning back.

Ayla stroked the baby's cheek. She peered into his face, trying to predict how his life would unfold. Would he be thin like his Momma or stocky like his Daddy? Would he smile easily or be angry all the time? Would he keep his blue eyes and grow caramel-colored hair? Ayla shivered. So many questions. So many answers she'd never know.

Maybe it was better. Maybe it was better riding off on the Harley with Mack and forgetting everything? Moeda would be left behind and Mack would be in front. The baby would be adopted by a rich family and everyone would live happily ever after. She remembered what the voice had told her.

Wrap him in the cloth to keep him warm, but make sure you see his face. You don't want to cover his face.

Ayla rewrapped the newborn in the red checked tablecloth from Pizza Baas – the same one Mack had used in Bear Mountain. She wondered if Sal ever missed it. She gently placed the baby into the picnic basket and watched him for a moment. Then she closed the top.

Ayla retrieved the crumpled napkin and pen that she had hidden beneath the mattress. She wanted to write a note. She hesitated. What do you say to a baby you'll never see again?

She began by choosing a name. It couldn't be just any name. It had to be biblical. The baby would need divine strength. Ayla waited for the name to magically drift into her head. Nothing. She mentally scanned the characters from her Sunday Bible School.

Hiram – the chief architect of Solomon's temple, free-born and noble.

Too weird.

Peter – one of Christ's apostles.

Too much like Peter Pan.

Elijah – the prophet.

Too ancient.

The name popped into her head.

Joshua.

Moses' prodigy. Joshua was the only Israelite allowed by God to approach Mount Sinai with Moses. A military man, Joshua became Moses' assistant, spy, and eventually leader of the Israelites, blessed with a lifetime of invincibility. The Bible said he lived a long and honorable life, dying at the age of one hundred and ten.

Perfect – Joshua was a strong leader who lived a long and productive life. Her baby would be a rich and powerful man. Maybe like his grandfather. If the baby's new mother didn't like the name she could call him Josh.

Satisfied, Ayla wrote the note.

The shadows deepened. Outside, the wind kicked up, howling like feral cats. She lifted the top of the basket and looked at the baby. He stirred. Ayla took the note and pinned it to the red checkered tablecloth.

"Now, what do I want for you?" Ayla asked Joshua, as if he could answer.

She took a deep breath.

"I want you to be a rock star," she giggled.

No. Too many drugs.

"I want you to be a businessman."

No. She thought of Sal.

"I want you to be a doctor."

No. Too bloody.

"I want you to be your true self."

Ayla shivered.

Your true self. Something I could never be.

"It's time," Mack interrupted. He glanced at the baby in the basket and read the note. "Joshua," he mumbled.

Ayla watched him. Her hands trembled – she didn't know what Mack would do next. Would he kill them or honor their deal? Her throat was thick with tears. She was afraid to speak. She bit her lip so Mack couldn't see her cry.

"Good-looking guy," Mack commented.

For a moment, Ayla thought she heard something in his voice. Something that said, "let's keep the kid." She segued into another movie – her, Mack and Joshua on the Harley, riding into the sunset, a happy family and . . .

"Don't get any ideas," Mack warned. "I'm dropping this bastard off with the cops. That's the deal. The *done* deal."

Ayla shifted her eyes to Joshua, committing his face to memory. *What am I doing?* A voice cried in her head. *What am I really doing?*

Ayla looked at Mack.

I love him. Not this baby.

She closed the top of the basket and offered it to Mack. Mack took it from her hands.

"As soon as I get back, we're gone."

"Done, just like we agreed."

"Done."

Mack tucked the basket under his tattooed arm as if he was carrying a football. And he was gone.

Ayla waited until she heard the Harley rev up. She listened to the roar slowly fade in the distance. She let the tears flow, surprised by her powerful emotions. It's only a baby, she told herself. I can have lots of them. I can only have one Mack.

She struggled to her feet. Everything hurt – she was so tired, sore, and strangely empty. She patted her belly as if to remind herself that Joshua was gone, down another road. It was time to pack up and head down *her* road. Time to be with Mack.

Joshua was on his own.

Ayla gathered her stuff. There wasn't much – there would never be much again. She slipped on an oversized tee shirt that covered her still-swollen belly. Mack would be back soon. They would head out without Joshua. She didn't know where they were going but that was okay. Mack would take care of her.

She left the bloody towels on the mattress. A week later one of the druggies from upstairs noticed the smell. He came through the unlocked back door and stared at the mess.

"That's why they fled," the druggie said to the stench. "Someone was murdered here."

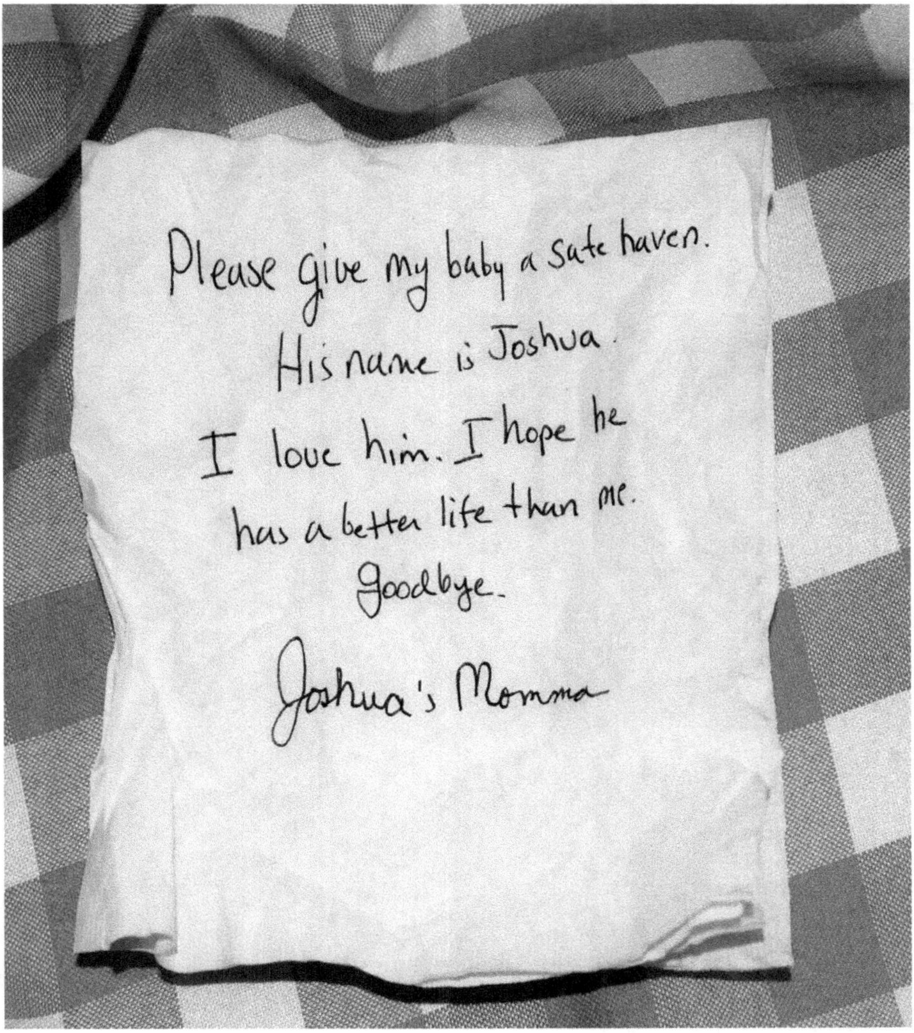
Please give my baby a safe haven.
His name is Joshua.
I love him. I hope he
has a better life than me.
Goodbye.
Joshua's Momma

Mack

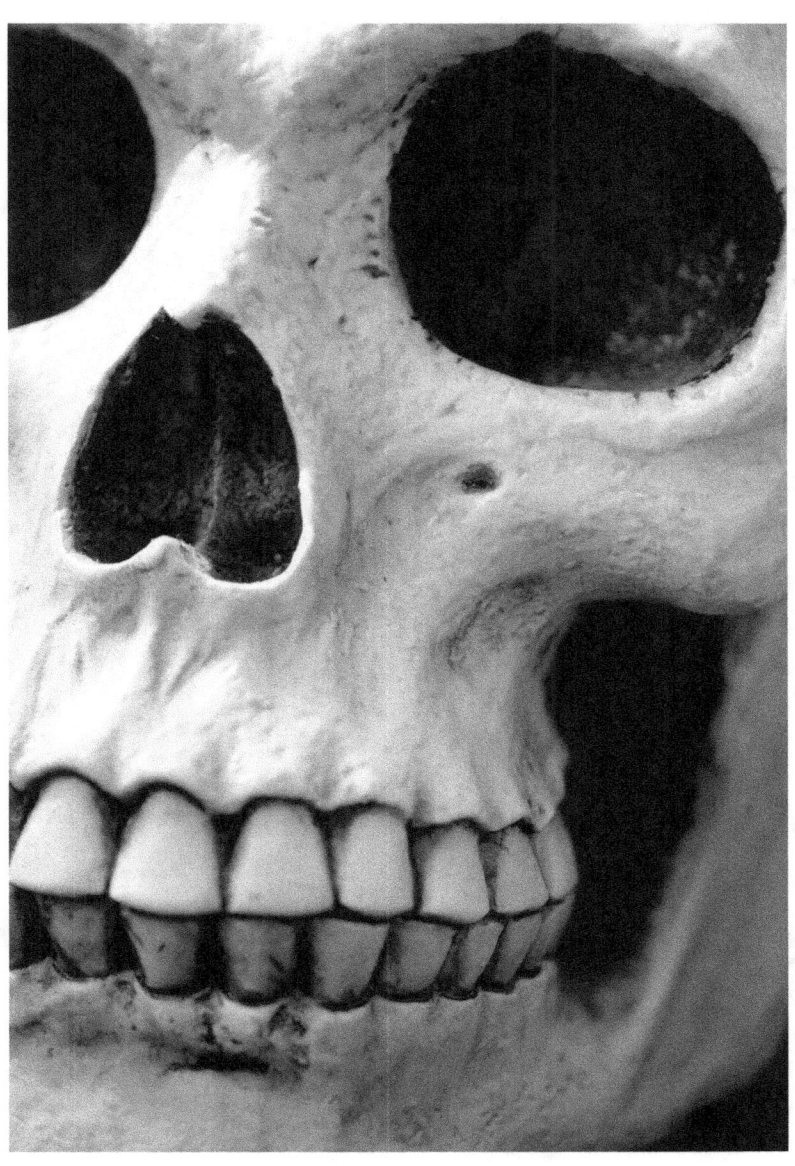

1

Mack left when Ayla's labor began. He didn't want to hear it. He also had some business to finish before they left Long Island.

He strapped his hunter combat knife to his belt, beneath his black leather jacket. It was an old friend – a good weapon, with a six-inch blade, razor point, shiny oxide finish, and high-impact handle. The knife was for killing – Mack had used it many times before.

The knife was made in the United States. Mack preferred to buy American products.

Mack headed to the sagging shed in the backyard where he kept his Harley. He liked the shed – it was a perfect place to keep his bike safe – the main reason for choosing the basement apartment.

Mack heard Ayla's screams. Faint, but clear.

"Bitch deserves it," he said out loud to no one. "She shouldn't have gotten knocked up."

He tenderly pulled the Harley from the shed and closed the door behind. He put on his helmet, climbed on the bike, and revved the engines, leaving Ayla to her labor.

Her cries had no effect on him, as he steered along the side of the house and onto the street. Maybe the druggies upstairs would care? Ayla had brought this shit on herself, and now she was paying the price.

Mack turned north on South Bayview Avenue to Sunrise Highway. He drove slowly so no one would notice him. By the time someone put the pieces together – if ever – they'd be long gone, headed west with his gang, no destination in mind. The baby would be done – today's business done – and Mack would lead the pack, military-style, to better grounds.

It only took him a few minutes to reach his destination.

The timing was perfect. There were only two people in the Pizza Baas. It would be a while until rush hour began and the commuters appeared. He parked in the Long Island Railroad lot, secured his bike, and went to the back door. Ayla had told him a long time ago that the door was always open, offering free entry to anything he wanted. He quietly slipped into the storeroom. Assholes always forgot to lock storeroom doors. Mack chuckled. It *had* been a good gig.

The storeroom was a maze of pipes, electric cables, and corrugated aluminum, dimly lit beneath a caged industrial light like the one in Mack's basement apartment. One wall was filled with shelves of cheap supplies – tomato sauce, oil, pasta, flour, and spices. It was dirty and dark; the owner was too cheap to burn bright lights.

Mack waited in the shadows, behind the door that opened into the joint. He could be a very patient man.

Sal will be sorry soon enough.

There were a few voices up front – customers chowing down and leaving through the front door. Finally, the only people Mack heard were the pimply teenager behind the cash register and Sal.

Mack hated Sal. He allowed Ayla to do him because she got free food and stole money from the register. The soft, middle-aged man had no right to take what was Mack's. Maybe, if he asked, Mack would have allowed it. Even watched. Sal never asked and Mack imagined his soft, fat fingers pawing her breasts and fingering her while spittle sprayed from his lips, and barely-contained grunts echoed in the storeroom.

Yeah. The man had to go.

It didn't take long. Sal opened the door and waddled into the storeroom, scratching his crotch.

Thinking of my bitch.

Mack smashed the door against him. Sal froze, shocked. Mack aimed a direct blow to his chest, over the heart. He didn't want to kill Sal that easily, only stun him into submission.

Staggering, Sal fell to his knees. Mack kicked the door closed and grabbed him from behind, pressing the hunter combat knife to his jugular.

"Yell," Mack growled, "and I'll kill you."

Sal squirmed but said nothing.

"Do you know what I want?"

Sal shook his head.

"My Bitch has been doing you without my permission. I don't like that."

"Mack?" Sal asked hoarsely. Sal couldn't see Mack's face.

"Who the hell do you think it is, fat boy?"

"I . . . I didn't know," Sal stuttered. "I didn't know you would be upset . . ."

"I don't care what you knew. You made her *do* you."

"I'm sorry." He started to babble, tears bursting from his eyes. "I didn't mean . . . take anything you want. Money. Pizza. I don't want to die."

Mack laughed. "Why would I want any of your shit?"

"Please," Sal begged. "I don't want to die. I have a wife . . . children . . ."

"Too late for that."

"Noooooo," Sal wailed. "I won't ever let her . . ."

Mack laughed and thrust the hunter combat knife into his right carotid artery. Blood spurted like a fountain from his neck. Then he punched the knife around, through his jugular, trachea, and left carotid, jiggling the knife until it made a ragged, raw edge that mangled the skin.

Someone had told Mack that it only took five seconds to bleed out after a cut like that.

He was dead right.

2

Mack let the body drop to the floor, took a deep breath, and savored the scent of fresh blood.

"I did you a favor," he grinned at Sal.

The soft, middle aged man stared up at him. His throat was completely open, his head almost decapitated. Blood pooled on the storeroom floor, saturating the mouse droppings. Sal made an interesting gurgling sound.

"No one," Mack stared at Sal impassively, "fucks with me."

Sal bled out.

Satisfied, Mack wiped the blood off his knife with a red checked cloth and slipped the weapon back into the sheath on his belt.

Job well done.

Mack ambled into the front of the pizzeria, leaving Sal and the storeroom behind. There were no customers.

"Nobody here?" Mack asked pleasantly, glancing at the terrified teenager behind the cash register.

The kid nodded.

"Pizza," Mack demanded.

The kid's hands shook as he served the slice. Mack stood at the counter and ate it slowly, making sure the kid watched. He left part of the slice on the plate, plucked a napkin from the metal holder, and wiped his mouth.

"This is what your boss looks like now." Mack grinned, pointing at the slice.

The kid's eyes bugged; he was too terrified to speak.

"You get the picture?"

The kid shook his head.

"Say it," Mack growled.

"I gggggggget it," the kid gurgled.

"Good. Very good. I won't hurt you. All you do when the cops come is say you never saw anything. You don't know who was in the storeroom."

Mack smiled kindly. He went to the door and flipped the sign to "closed." "If you happen to forget . . . I'll be back with the guys and . . ." He laughed. "You'll look just like your boss."

The biker sighed happily, and left the pizzeria. It was time to get back to Ayla.

3

There was one last job.

Ayla was packing up her stuff. The guys were waiting for him near the entrance to Meadowbrook Parkway. Mack was ready to move on – as soon as he took care of the basket with the kid.

He strapped the basket onto the Harley the same way he carried it to their picnic on Bear Mountain. He drove down Merrick Road to the Seaford Police Station and turned down a side street, parking next to a rusted construction dumpster. He was careful not to break any laws.

Mack didn't want to be seen . . . just in case . . . just in fucking case.

He peeked into the basket. The baby was very quiet. Mack touched the kid's chest to make sure he was breathing.

Yeah, he was alive. Just very quiet. Fucking babies.

For a moment, something inside Mack worked its way to the surface.

This kid is mine.

Joshua. Mack rolled the name over his tongue like a smoldering cigar. Joshua. Mack knew about the others. The women had told him; he threatened them; and they all went away. He was younger then. Much younger. Didn't want any part of the bitches.

Joshua was different. Mack *saw* the kid. He looked like Ayla – and the Bitch had gotten under Mack's skin. Man, she was only a kid herself. He was old enough to be her father.

Suddenly the years roared through Mack's head, like a convoy of bikes destined for nowhere. What was it all about? Why did it happen? He glanced at the tattoos that covered his arms – permanent cartoons carved into his skin. It was so important twenty years ago. And now?

Mack shook his head. There was no room for mental chatter. No room for a baby. The only thing he could give was a few grudging inches for Ayla.

Done deal.

The bitch. Why did she have to get knocked up?

He licked his lips.

"There isn't enough room for Ayla *and* Joshua," he said out loud, to no one.

For a brief moment, Mack reviewed the anger, violence, and transience of his life. Was it all worth it? A half century on the planet and what did he have to show for it?

It was a brief window that opened and closed quickly. Mack was not about to regret anything. He liked his life.

Mack stroked the basket, as if preparing for a kill.

It was tough to walk into a police station. Mack had spent too many years on the other side of cops. He didn't like them; they didn't like him. No trust. It suited him just fine. Only this time he needed them. Mack winced.

Yeah, I need the fuckers.

The only way to move on was to dump the kid and keep Ayla.

The only way.

Mack hated the weakness in him that emerged when he turned fifty. He hid it from everyone, threatening with his fists, snarling at the guys, displaying his Nazi Iron Eagle like a piece aimed at the world. No one knew that age had sapped swaths of energy and courage; that he needed Ayla because she was young and terrified of him. Yeah, he knocked her around to show who was boss. That was just the way things were meant to be. Maybe he even *cared*? Fuck, what did that mean anyway? No one – including Ayla – would ever suspect. All he had to do was *pretend* he loved her, and that was enough. She'd stick around. And stand away from the Moeda bitch who would turn him in for rape if she got the chance.

No one would get the chance.

Get rid of the kid and we're outta here.

Mack looked at the dumpster. Suddenly an idea filled his head, spreading like the pool of blood beneath Sal's body.

Leave the kid there.

No one would know. The kid would die and be better off for it. He'd lie to Ayla and she would be happy. The game would be done.

Something stopped him. Years later, Mack would question why he went into the cop station instead of throwing out the kid. Was it a moment of weakness? Was it the promise he made to Ayla? Or did he actually *want* to give the little bastard a chance at life? There was no answer. He unstrapped the basket, headed toward the police station, and paused in front of the Safe Haven sign.

Safe Babies. Safe Place. Safe Haven.

He took a deep breath. Slowly, he climbed the steps and entered the station. It was small, cool, and brightly-lit. Fortunately, the place was quiet. An angry-looking bitch with a black eye sat on a bench. There were screens in the back room, and a dispatcher sitting at a table behind a mike. The place was painted in notices – everything from Safe Haven to local, state, and national *Most Wanted* posters.

Mack walked up to the desk and put the basket down in full sight. He knew that he had to leave the kid in someone's hands.

The Duty Officer, a big guy with a belly that strained the buttons on his uniform, stared at the basket, and then at Mack.

No one spoke.

4

Mack took a deep breath. "Safe Haven?" he asked cryptically. "I want to leave this kid with you." He opened the top. The cop peered in, his eyes narrowed, and his mouth caved into a frown.

"Are you a representative for the mother?" The cop asked slowly.

"Yeah."

There was something about the way Mack tilted his head and furrowed his forehead that triggered a cold chill in the Duty Officer.

"Are you the . . . grandfather?" The cop asked.

"Fuck no," Mack retorted.

"The father?"

"I thought Safe Haven meant not identifying yourself," Mack snarled. "No questions."

"Are you representing the Birth Mother?" The Duty Officer tried again.

Mack sniffed. "What does it look like?"

The Duty Officer took a deep breath. "You don't have to reveal your identity or the mother's identity, as long as the child is unharmed."

"He's not even a fucking day old," Mack sneered. "Who had time to beat him?"

The cop frowned. "Would you – or the mother – be willing to supply a medical history? That's voluntary of course."

"No way. Just the kid."

"I'm going to give you a packet. It's completely up to you – or the Birth Mother – to fill it out. It includes a medical questionnaire, self-addressed stamped envelope, and information about the program. It tells you about the law – how parents' privacy is protected, legal rights . . ."

The cop handed Mack an envelope.

"I don't give a fuck about this shit," Mack said. "Take the kid and I'm gone." He slid the basket closer to the Duty Officer.

"Can I ask a few questions before you go?"

Mack narrowed his eyes suspiciously.

"You don't have to answer them," the Duty Officer added.

Mack was silent.

"How old is the . . ." The cop read the note in the basket. "Joshua."

"One day," Mack said quickly.

"Time and place of birth?"

Mack shook his head.

"Do you know whether there are any . . . health problems in the Birth Mother or Father?"

"We're fine," Mack snarled.

"Are there any affiliations to an Indian tribe?"

"We're no fucking Indians," Mack hissed.

"Is there any other information about Joshua's medical, social, and family history?"

"I'm outta here," Mack scowled. He grabbed the envelope and turned his back to the Duty Officer.

"Wait," the Duty Officer called, knowing it was useless.

Mack raced through the door, down the steps, and escaped into the streets. He clutched the knife on his belt, resisting the urge to pull the weapon from its sheath. Mack was convinced someone would follow him. He paused and scanned the street. There was no one. He slunk back to his Harley, took a deep breath, tossed the Safe Haven Information Pack into the dumpster, and headed back to Ayla.

He looked at the sky. A storm was brewing, headed straight for Long Island. The ominous black clouds were moving in, covering the sun. Time to get going.

Mack and Ayla were gone within the hour, followed by Mack's gang.

5

Duty Officer James McBride stared at the biker's back. There was nothing he could do. The law said that parents could leave – remain anonymous – as long as the baby was safe, unharmed, and not abused.

McBride peered into the basket. "Who are you little one?" He asked softly. "No one – including you – will ever know."

At least the baby was alive, McBride thought. Too many babies were abandoned in dumpsters, left to die, shaken, starved to death, or butchered by a jealous boyfriend. This little guy would have a life and a future, unlike the others.

The baby's eyes fluttered open.

"Blue eyes, eh," McBride said softly. "Maybe you'll keep them."

McBride knew babies – he had four kids of his own.

"What do you have there?" A voice said over his shoulder.

"Safe Haven," McBride explained.

Officer Paula Tinto looked into the basket. "Poor guy," she said sadly. Her straight brown hair was pulled back into a ponytail at the nape of her neck. She touched the baby's palm, and his tiny hand curled around her index finger. "He's small. Very small." A few strands of hair fell across her concerned face.

Tinto read the note on the red checked tablecloth. "Joshua. That's a good name for a baby. Joshua," she repeated, turning the sound over in her mouth. "Joshua is a newborn, McBride, not more than a day old."

McBride nodded. He didn't need Tinto to tell him that.

Tinto bent down and went through the papers beneath the desk. "Protocol," she said, "for Safe Haven." She slammed the manual on the desk. The baby jumped. Tinto gently removed Joshua from the basket, tightening the red checked tablecloth, and cradling him in her arms.

"You're not supposed to do that," McBride said.

Tinto ignored him.

"Ahhhhhhh baby," she cooed. "Ahhhhhhh baby."

McBride glanced at the manual. It felt like a book of life – the story of Joshua. He was suddenly overcome with sadness. The kid was just an abandoned newborn without a momma.

Tinto acknowledged McBride's reaction in her eyes.

McBride recited the procedure out loud. "Request medical assistance – an ambulance. They'll bring the baby to the ER, where the pediatrician in charge will take over. Joshua's age will be determined, along with his health. Then they'll put him in neonatal isolation to make sure he's not contagious. Child Protective Services will be notified, and take custody. The hospital will keep him a few days, in case the mother changes her mind. If no one shows up," McBride sighed, "he'll be put in a foster home where hopefully, the parents will adopt him after the court formally declares him available."

"Ahhhhhhh baby," Tinto cooed, "this is not a great way to start life."

Tinto shook her head. There was an odd comfort in the rules. They told the police what to do, where Joshua was going, and in a veiled way, his future. It was cold and black-and-white. Everyone could ignore the shocks of infantile grief as if they never existed. What does a baby *feel* anyway? Baby Joshua would move on immersed in the system; McBride would go home to his four kids; and Tinto would take her 8 year old twins out for pizza. Hugs would be a fraction longer than usual, but no one would notice. Tomorrow, the world would go back to normal.

Tinto glanced out the window. A storm was brewing outside, headed straight for Long Island. The ominous black clouds were moving in, covering the sun. The words came, unbidden.

I hope that's not an omen for baby Joshua.

6

The sounds assault me. They crawl into my body and shock every cell. Quiet and cozy is wrenched forever from my world. I plunge into harsh, deafening chaos with a wild cacophony of sensations.

I'm alone.

I know she's gone, left me to fend with strangers, and ripped me from her soul. Please come back. Please don't leave me. I need you. We're supposed to be one. Don't you know that? Don't you remember? A strange voice breaks in.

Who are you little one?

The sound is deep and threatening; ugly and guttural. Terror floods me.

Who are you?

As if I can answer. I open my eyes and light pierces, bolts to my soul. So bright. So hurtful.

Blue eyes, eh? Maybe you'll keep them.

The voice softens, but not nearly enough. There's no gentleness or familiarity. Just pain. Then I hear something else. Softer. Sweeter. I shut my eyes.

Poor guy.

Fingers curl around my body. Arms raise me from my cocoon. It's so cold. I shiver. I'm pressed against a warm, strange breast. That feels better. Do I hear the thump of a heartbeat? The rhythm struggles to drown out the other sounds. I open my eyes slowly, cautiously.

He's small. Very small.

The face isn't frightening. I relax a bit.

Joshua. That's a good name for a baby.

I like the sweet, rolling tones.

Safe Haven.

The words have no meaning, but arms and voice shelter me from the light and noise. I close my eyes again and listen.

Ahhhhhh baby.

The voice is different, but the sounds are similar. The terror eases.

Ahhhhhh baby.

Where is she? What happens now? Why does she leave? Why does she hate me?

The questions linger, burrowing deep inside my brain. I have no words to ask the question out loud; no way to cry the terror.

Help me.

Momma.

Please. Come. Back.

She's part of me, and now she's gone. What have I done? Why won't she come back?

The thoughts become part of me; fear cradles my heart. I'm different and alone. Momma is gone. Momma takes part of me with her and leaves the other to linger, hurt, torn, and terrified.

Why Momma?

Why?

I drift into numbing sleep.

Ahhhhhh baby.

Kiran

1

Kiran hovered in her space, deep within the antiseptic building that housed the Nassau County Department of Social Services – better known as DSS. The white building screamed Kafkaesque civil service; surrounded by a flat, sprawling parking lot where people fought for space.

She was like a lone tree at sunset; her against a world of files, numbers, and bureaucratic codes. Kiran stared at the paperwork on her desk. It was stacked haphazardly in piles of folders, envelopes, stapled forms, and sticky notes. Just looking at it made her frown. There was so much; it always kept coming in an endless supply of tragedies. Ironically, electronic data *increased* the amount of forms, requiring a longer, thicker paper trail for every action.

"Just in case," her supervisor said daily. "We have to protect ourselves. Cover our backs."

Kiran hated those words. There were too many just-in-cases. She shuddered. Lives had been reduced to forms and procedures; stories were told in quickly-scrawled reports; people survived in a file cabinet or computer, protected by passwords that failed. Even for Kiran, a young, optimistic social worker, the DSS – Services to Children and Families, was hell. Her desk was never clear, her work never done, her days flooded with too many crises that could be deadly if missed or ignored. Adoptions and foster care sounded simple, but it was actually a morass of trouble, with kids seized from families, parents arrested, emergency housing scarce . . . the list was endless. She stared at the latest stack of stories, kids threatened, abused, neglected, wrenched from homes where parents didn't or couldn't care. When she first began this job, she had to learn *not to care*. It was too painful to bring home the stories, see the faces, and let the kids enter her world. No one could survive the sheaves of pain.

Kiran was no exception.

Kiran ran her fingers through her hair. She was an attractive woman, with large blue eyes enhanced by expensive make-up and skilled stylists. Although she worked at DSS, Kiran wore worn-looking designer clothing to make sure she didn't stand out among her peers or clients. It didn't work; Kiran had the speech and bearing that refused to blend into a sterile social service office. She was the modern version of a turn-of-the-century Settlement House worker; a wealthy philanthropic women with a social conscience.

Even rarer today.

"You won't survive," her supervisor advised Kiran when she first started at DSS. "You're too soft. The only way is to build a glass wall around you – a cocoon – where you can see everything, hear everything, feel everything, but not let anything in."

Kiran refused to accept those terms, but after months of crying, anger, and frustration, she complied. She methodically erected her glass wall, allowing her to help without being touched. Gradually, the nightmares waned and enraged parents withdrew. Broken homes, filled with dirt, vermin, and cruelty, were relegated to the daytime.

Kiran was in the trenches – a social worker committed to changing the world from the bottom up. It was so simple that she felt ridiculous saying the words.

Change the world. Make a difference.

They were clichés that belonged to university courses on social policy. Kiran should have known the truth. She should have accepted the improbability of change; should have surrendered to the inevitable. The Albert Ellis term flashed in her mind. Ellis was the father of Rational Emotive Behavior Theory. He referred to "should" as *musterbation* – where an individual believes he or she has an obligation to do something differently from what is presently being done. If one doesn't do what she *should*, the result is feeling wrong and guilty – a moral failure. Kiran smiled. Maybe it would be easier being a psychopath who doesn't feel anything.

Kiran had trouble conquering her *shoulds*. She refused to be defeated by the enormity of her mission; refused to be defeated by the pessimism of the previous generation. Kiran was determined to chip away, little by little, at the horrors that clung to the poor, abused, and underserved.

If I help one child, that's enough.

It was never enough. One child was preceded by hundreds and followed by even more. There was so much need that Kiran grew numb from the relentless demand.

Occasionally, the folder of a child would end up on her desk, crying out louder than the others. Kiran looked at the note on her pile of paperwork.

He was that child.

She had read his file, already thick for his young life, but it was the note, scrawled on a wrinkled paper napkin and pinned to a scrap of red checked cloth, that caught her heart. It was in girlish handwriting that reached out to her like hands begging for help

She didn't know Baby Joshua. She hadn't even seen him, yet the questions and *shoulds* flew out of control. Kiran felt a connect.

Who is Joshua? Why does he need me so badly?

That was the way it happened. The glass wall held strong until an imperfection appeared, like a pebble hitting a car's windshield. It burrowed in the glass until the cracks radiated and Kiran's defenses collapsed.

There were too many of them. The little boy who crept in, his arms and legs scarred from cigarette burns. A mom, whose face was disfigured by daily beatings from a drug addicted husband, wailing in primal agony as her children were taken away. A 12-year old girl, her arms twisted from breaks, clinging to the dog her father, and rapist, had killed.

And now, Joshua.

2

Kiran stared at the note and was flooded with memories.

Her parents had warned her not to go into social work – certainly not to work for DSS. They raised her in a large, expensive home in Garden Village – one of the wealthiest towns on Long Island. The 6-bedroom/6-bathroom home was set back from the street, partially concealed by old, graceful trees, with a sprawling front lawn. The backyard held a pool, tennis courts, a small guest house, and fully furnished patio.

Garden Village was known for its luxury and silent majority. Years ago, Jews were openly denied the right to build a local synagogue or become members in the Garden Village Country Club. Hispanics, Afro-Americans, and Gays were systematically shunned. Her town was an enclave of white, wealthy Christians who, in their political correctness, denied discrimination. Kiran knew otherwise.

No one from Garden Village went into Social Work with the poor or abused unless they were political appointees.

Her parents didn't get it – they were jaded, soft, and indifferently accepted the injustices of the world. She could hear their voices.

"I told you – you're not made for this kind of work . . ."

"This work is for different people."

"You're too refined; you live in a different world."

It was very clear, years ago, when she told them her intention to pursue social work, how much they hated the idea.

The three had been sitting in *The Grille*, a dark, candle-lit brasserie which featured delicately seasoned lobster tails expertly paired with a *Corton-Charlemagne Grand Cru*. Her fraternal twin brother, Robert, refused to join them. He was off on another adventure, exploring the elite of New York with his film crew. She envied his freedom; his ability to do whatever he chose and not care about it. It was always about Robert – what *he* wanted and where *he* wandered. She was the polar opposite of her twin – serious and ethical.

The wine rested in a silver bucket on a stand next to the table. Instead of music, voices in hushed, polite conversation serenaded them. It was a good spot to be seen; upscale dining in *The Grille at Garden Village Country Club*, members only, meant something.

Father ate dinner between an endless parade of firm handshakes, greeting each person with the smile Kiran detested. Father relished the attention as much as the wine.

"Thank you. Thank you. Thank you," The Senator said pleasantly, his voice dripping like contaminated honey. Everyone wanted The Senator on their side.

Kiran rolled her eyes at Mother. They were used to it.

"I'm going to change the world," Kiran added matter-of-factly, after a small group of local investment bankers had pumped Father's hand and retreated to their table by the window. "Make it a better place. That's why I decided to major in social work."

There was a long, pregnant silence.

Father looked at another table – a collection of pharmaceutical executives – and smiled pleasantly.

"Can't you be a doctor?" Mother asked.

"Or a lawyer," Father frowned, rubbing his forehead, and returning momentarily to their conversation.

Kiran laughed. She loved her parents, but they didn't get her. She wasn't doctor or lawyer material – she was meant to go out and work with *real* people.

"I am what I am, Father," she said. He didn't hear her. Another group had come to greet him.

Years later, with a Masters in Social Work and a job at DSS, they still didn't get it. Kiran chuckled. She wasn't angry with her parents. She knew who they were and what they believed about their world. She smiled inside.

What would they think about Morgan?

Kiran had never introduced her boyfriend Morgan to her parents. They weren't particularly fond of biracial relationships. How would Morgan look in *The Grille*? Mother and Father would shudder to know that the man, who slept with their daughter between his shifts, was a fireman and not a corporate attorney or business mogul.

She sipped at the wine. It was a splendid white with rich buttery and fruit flavors – and notes of cinnamon, vanilla, and honey.

"How about an industrial psychologist?" Father had conceded. "I can get you into a doctoral program."

"No," Kiran retorted. "That's not what I want to do. I want to help people. I want to make a difference in the world."

Mother sniffed. "You'll change your mind."

Father continued. "There are easier ways to make a difference." He paused. "Look at me."

Kiran had shivered at his monotone. Father was very far from the warm-and-fuzzy type. Kiran forgave him for his hard, plastic nature and uncompromising style. She knew he loved her in his own way.

If everyone else in the state loved the man, so could she.

3

Now, after four years of undergraduate, two years of graduate school, professional licensing, and supervision, Kiran had a job that was dirtier than most. DSS was pure bureaucracy, struggling to survive in an epidemic of poverty, crumbling families, domestic violence, government cutbacks, and an unending spiral of clients. Each worker was drowning in cases and paperwork; at risk for missing *the one* that made the newspapers because a parent or boyfriend murdered a kid.

Kiran looked at the note from Joshua's Momma. The Safe Haven baby had already been saved from that fate. He was the lucky one.

Baby Joshua Doe.

Kiran was drawn to Joshua in a macabre way. It was as if he screamed at her, sending invisible tentacles to seize her attention. Kiran was a woman of science, and yet she heard a silent voice inside, almost paranormal, begging.

Look at me. Listen. I'm Joshua.

Kiran ran her fingers over the note as if touching it would give her some clues to Joshua's story. It was cold. Kiran thought about the words:

> *Please give my baby a safe haven. His name is Joshua.*
> *I love him. I hope he has a better life than me. Goodbye.*
> *Joshua's Momma*

Why did it send chills down her back? Was it another imperfection in her safety glass?

Kiran took a deep breath. She asked the obvious questions out loud. Who are you, Joshua's Momma? Why did you abandon him? Kiran tried to analyze the handwriting. It was large and childlike, suggesting that Joshua's mother was probably a kid. No surprise. Most abandoned babies in Safe Haven were the children of young, unmarried, physically healthy women pregnant for the first time. The mothers were desperate – they simply didn't know what to do. They denied their pregnancies, isolated themselves, sought no prenatal care, and made no plans for the birth or care of themselves or their babies. Contrary to popular opinion, most of them didn't have an alcohol or substance abuse problem, a medical issue easily detected in the hospital. Joshua didn't have to go through withdrawal during his first days in the world.

Perhaps the most revealing fact about Baby Joshua Doe's mother was that he was *alive*. Newborns faced the greatest risk of murder during the first *day* of life. Joshua survived; his mother cared enough not to leave him in a place where he would have died – a dumpster, trash bin, dark alley, warehouse, or public bathroom.

Kiran shivered. She tried to imagine a newborn stuffed in a dumpster, and suffocated by mounds of garbage. It was incomprehensible. Joshua's Momma was better than *that*.

4

Kiran wove a fantasy about Joshua and his Momma.
A highly-rated television reality drama.
Momma wanted the best for her child, but couldn't provide it. The child was destined to be born. Kiran, the rescuer, was destined to protect him. Karma. The tale emerged from her love of literature rather than the reality of social work. It was a fantasy destined to be wrecked by the system.

Maybe she could write a happy ending?

Kiran fingered the note. *Safe Haven*. That's what the Birth Mother wanted – a safe haven for her baby.

Why, Joshua's Momma? Why did you leave him?

Were you raped? Was it incest? Was he in the way, the child of a man other than your boyfriend or the man you lived with? Did he interfere with your plans? Was it a mistake you were too young to correct? Was Safe Haven the only way to save his life?

Kiran frowned. She would never know. Even worse, Joshua would never know. All her years of education, professional training, experience, and instinct told Kiran that it was a terrible way to start life.

I'll change that.

The truth challenged her resolve. Kiran thought of the kids that shuffled through her office. There was the baby boy who was born on a rock, in the middle of a park and the infant girl found with her mentally ill mother under a dirty bridge. She remembered the brother and sister, 8 and 10 years old, who had been in 6 different foster homes, and the teenage boy who was aging out because his abusive parents had refused to relinquish custody, thus denying any hope of adoption. She reminded herself of the good stories, like the foster family who had 2 biological children, 6 Down's Syndrome children, and devoted themselves to providing a home for unwanted kids. The stories, books, articles and ongoing sound bytes were endless. There were even some foster moms who practiced "adoptive breastfeeding" to enhance bonding with the babies placed in their care. Yet there were never enough homes to keep up with the supply of needy kids.

Kiran recalled the foster mom who had spent 20 years taking care of kids until a crack-addicted newborn was put under her protection. He had so many challenges, physical problems, learning disabilities, developmental issues . . . the list was endless. Step-by-step, this foster mom embraced her charge and when he was released for adoption, welcomed him permanently into her family, even though she lost his monthly stipend.

Kiran sighed. The stories were tragic and uplifting; good parents and bad parents; good kids and irretrievably damaged kids. They were the best and worst of humankind. Nothing was ever benign. It was a series of human dramas, played out in the forms on her desk and the records in her computer – the struggles of children who craved safe *forever homes* like normal kids craved *American Girl Dolls* and *Monster Trucks*. The numbers were chilling – more than half a million kids lived in foster homes across the country, with an average of three *different* placements in a two – three year period. Each year, only 50-60,000 foster kids were adopted while another nearly 130,000 kids aged out of the system. It took up to 6 months to terminate parental rights, while only 30% of foster kids ever returned home. The outcomes were equally grim – foster care kids became runaways, street kids, substance abusers, homeless, mentally ill, incarcerated . . . the list was horrific. Some kids *were* successful; too many fell between the cracks of a weak and stressed system.

Baby Joshua Doe was another name on a very long list. He was now entered into the system with nowhere to go.

Kiran searched her lists, spoke with her colleagues, and desperately looked for a foster home. Every place was filled – most overcrowded, near or exceeding legal limits. Taking on a newborn required time and energy, straining demands made on busy foster parents. She searched for a foster/adoption home, but there was no one left on her list. There was no choice. Joshua's first home would be an emergency placement until something more permanent could be found. Thirty days at best.

That was no surprise, either. Most babies were in three different foster homes in their first year of life.

"What's going to happen to you, Joshua?" Kiran said out loud. Did you know what you were really doing, Joshua's Momma?

She stared at the note as if expecting an answer. The napkin didn't even flutter.

In an impulsive gesture that would last a lifetime, Kiran scrawled a few words on a note.

> Please keep birth note from Joshua's Momma
> with all records.
> Do not remove – Kiran

She stapled it to Baby Joshua's paperwork.

Kiran began Joshua's search for a forever home with Denise Fletcher. It was an emergency placement, and with luck, would become a permanent home. The Fletchers would not be able to resist the newborn; they would love him, mourn his tragic start, and embrace him in their family. They lived in an old, small, and cluttered house in a working class neighborhood where Joshua could grow up with a lot of other kids, noise, and fun.

5

One month later, Denise Fletcher opened the front door to her home. Kiran smiled pleasantly. Kiran *knew* that Denise would bond with Baby Joshua Doe and keep him, although she already had a house full of kids. The Fletchers were good people. Joshua would do well with them.

Kiran liked Denise. The woman worked hard, cared for the kids, and did her best. Unfortunately, her best wasn't always *the best*. Kiran had to keep close tabs on the house, never sure how much stress Denise could handle. The 38 year old woman had a good heart, and loved the kids, although she didn't always make the right decisions. She was somewhat limited in the psychology of foster kids, often making the incorrect assumption that if you give them love and kindness, they'll be fine.

Far from true.

"Sometimes," Kiran had told Denise, "they're not fine. Sometimes they're scared, abandoned, angry, abused . . . afraid to connect."

Denise had shrugged, humoring the DSS worker. What did Kiran know – she was young, without kids, not even married . . .

"And sometimes," Kiran added grimly. "It's genes."

Kiran recognized that there was some truth to the assessment. A job with DSS did not make her an expert on parenting - nor did her college degrees.

What do I know? What do I have to do to become an expert?

All her textbooks, her research, and her studies were not the same as living with these broken children.

"C'mon in," Denise said tiredly.

Kiran saw it immediately. The shadows under the eyes, glazed look, and forced smile told the story, along with a wrinkled blouse and jeans streaked with markers and food stains.

Denise was exhausted. Drained.

Kiran took a deep breath and paused.

Baby Joshua had crept under Kiran's skin, residing in a place that was dangerous for a DSS worker. Her own life was documented – Kiran had a family tree that stretched back hundreds of years into the early days of New York, filled with old, respected names that she could follow in textbooks. She grew up as the child of a political celebrity.

Joshua had nothing. He was a baby without a history.

Kiran followed Joshua's first placement carefully, spending extra time telephoning and encouraging Denise. She prayed that the Fletchers would adopt the newborn, raising him as one of their own. Kiran had constructed a scenario that was unlikely, considering what most foster children experienced. She had built it knowing that it had no real basis.

One look at Denise told Kiran that Joshua had not found his *forever home*.

"C'mon in," Denise repeated impatiently.

"New landscaping?" Kiran asked weakly, pointing to the Rhododendron next to the red brick stairs.

"Yeah, sure. Al did some work with Billy and Jake."

Billy and Jake. Their specs snapped through Kiran's head, like the stats on baseball players. Two boys, sibling pair, ages 9 and 11. Parents incarcerated for drug possession and sales. Custodial rights were not released, although both parents faced long sentences. The boys couldn't be adopted. They had lived with the Fletchers for two years, after being plucked from a dank, filthy apartment littered with drug paraphernalia. Dad had beaten them with broomsticks. Mom ignored them; numb from alcohol and her latest drug of choice. No relatives wanted custody. The Fletchers took them in and the boys were doing well. They made passing grades in school and got along with their peers. At home they were pleasant, never giving the Fletchers any problems. Kiran wondered why some kids survived the horrors of their childhoods and others did not.

"We all know about the bad seed," her supervisor had once told her. "But there's a good seed as well – forces inside a child that enable him or her to survive the horrors, rise above the neglect and sexual assaults, and grow into a functioning adult."

"Are you sure?" Kiran asked innocently.

"Very sure. Thank God for the good seeds. They give us hope."

And the bad seeds?

Kiran wondered if Billy and Jake were "good seeds" or whether they would explode when puberty took hold, as was the case with so many broken kids. Only time would tell. Things changed when hormones raged, even with the sweetest kids.

Denise frowned. "Kiran," she said sharply.

Kiran sighed. The good seeds were not predominant, but they still existed. Some were born. Others were nurtured. Perhaps the largest group occurred when genetics met the environment – where behaviors embedded in the brain were triggered by experience. Forces that lived in the cells and souls of some people were able to conquer what a dark world offered. Although Kiran had *not* grown up in an abusive environment, she knew that there were good and bad seeds among the privileged as well. Power, celebrity, and affluence were more likely to conceal true identities.

"Where are the kids now?" Kiran interrupted her thoughts, as she stepped into the house.

Denise's face brightened. "Billy and Jake are at a soccer game with Al. Wanda is a starter, so they went to cheer her on."

Wanda was the most recent addition to the house – a pretty eight year old waiting for her mother to complete rehabilitation for heroin addiction.

Denise frowned. "I couldn't go because of the baby."

She kicked a sack of toys and everything fell on the floor. Denise and Kiran stared at the mess. It said more about the Fletcher house than their words.

6

Kiran heard the bitterness in Denise's voice. She wanted out. Kiran looked around. The house was small and overcrowded, with Denise, Al, three foster kids, and a newborn. It was the norm rather than the exception. Good homes, like the Fletcher's, were usually overcrowded.

The house was cleaned for a home visit from DSS. A few toys were piled neatly in one corner; a big, well-used doll was placed strategically on the couch. It was too clean – no one could keep it that way with so many kids. Kiran closed her eyes and pictured what it would look like on a normal day, kids rushing, laughing, toys and sports stuff strewn throughout, a TV blasting . . .

The way a happy house should be.

Denise offered Kiran a seat on the worn beige couch. Kiran noticed a brown stain, tucked beneath the doll. Probably soda.

"Coffee?" Denise asked Kiran.

"No, thank you."

Denise nodded, sitting in a chair opposite Kiran. She ran her fingers through short, curly brown hair. "I don't know how to say this," Denise began, taking a deep breath. She licked her lips with the tip of her tongue.

Kiran waited, shifting into a therapeutic stance.

"You know I love kids," Denise continued. "I mean, some of the kids that aged out of here still visit . . . remember Jackie? She works downtown, still calls, and comes for dinner. Then there's Manuel, he's in the Navy and sends me postcards whenever he can."

"I know," Kiran stopped her. "You and Al are some of the best foster parents in the system."

Denise nodded solemnly. "Thank you. If I had a bigger house, I would double the number of kids."

Kiran agreed.

"This kid Joshua, he's different." Denise searched for words, but couldn't find them. "Different," she repeated softly.

"Different?"

Denise nodded. "He doesn't like me."

"How can a baby not like you? You're the gentlest person in . . ."

"He doesn't like me," Denise interrupted. "I *know.*"

"He's just an infant, Denise. You can't make judgments like that."

"I can," Denise gritted her teeth, "because I know."

"I don't . . ."

"Watch," Denise said fiercely.

She led Kiran into a closet-sized nursery crammed with a crib, changing table, drawers, and piles of baby paraphernalia. Kiran squeezed next to Denise and peered into the crib at the sleeping infant. Joshua was a beautiful baby, with pink cheeks, a heart-shaped mouth, and silky, caramel-colored hair. He was dressed in a soft blue sleeper and smelled like baby lotion.

"He's beautiful," Kiran whispered.

Denise shrugged. She bent over the crib and reached in to pick up Joshua. As soon as she touched him, Joshua's eyes flew open and his mouth made strange, repetitive movements, like sucking a bottle. Denise gently held him to her breast, cooing softly.

Joshua wailed – harsh, ear-splitting cries, flailing frantically as if trying to get away from her. His shrieks were heart-breaking. Denise changed his position, but the cries continued. She tried to fill his mouth with a pacifier, but he spit it out, furiously continuing his wails. Frustrated, Denise carefully placed him back on the mattress. As soon as she moved away, Joshua stopped crying.

The two women stared at the baby.

"He doesn't want to be held," Denise shook her head. "He doesn't want to eat and he can't suck well. Changing his diaper is an ordeal . . ."

Kiran gazed at Joshua.

What's wrong with you, little one?

"He never responds. He doesn't coo or smile. The kid fights everything."

Kiran shook her head.

"He's a beautiful baby," Denise added weakly. "I hope his new foster parents do better than me."

At that moment, the front door burst open and Al and the kids filled the house with excitement. Denise glanced at Kiran and left the nursery. Clearly, the foster mother was relieved to leave Joshua in Kiran's care.

Kiran watched from the doorway.

The kids hugged Denise, breathlessly telling the story about Wanda's winning goal. Al laughed and Denise grinned.

A happy family.

Except for the baby.

She glanced at Joshua. He showed no response to the excitement around him.

He was content to be left alone.

Although it was a sunny day, it felt like black clouds were moving in and an ominous storm was brewing.

It was time to find another home for Baby Joshua Doe.

7

Kiran couldn't sleep. She tossed in bed, amazed that Morgan slept so soundly.

Kiran and Morgan had been living together for a year. He was beautiful to look at – his cocoa skin was the color of a Starbuck's latte, his powerful body muscled and maintained with precision. Kiran was in love with him.

They lived in her upscale condo, *Lindbergh Towers,* on the edge of Garden Village and close to one of the largest shopping malls in America – Roosevelt Field. The mall was built on land that was once Hazelhurst Airfield; renamed Roosevelt Field in honor of Quentin, Theodore Roosevelt's son who was killed in World War I. It was most famous as the airfield where Charles Lindbergh began his historic 1927 solo trans-Atlantic Flight. In 1951 the airfield closed and five years later ground was broken for a shopping center. The only remnant of Lindbergh was the name of the condo and a plaque, placed beneath the mall escalator near the *Disney Store.*

Lindbergh Towers was a gated condo, close to history, filled with young entrepreneurs and professionals, up-and-coming designers, and adult children with wealthy parents. As a fireman, Morgan didn't quite fit into that category, but that never bothered anyone. Since 9/11, firemen were heroes. Morgan looked the role.

Kiran glanced at Morgan, sleeping next to her.

He's beautiful. Inside and out.

The condo boasted indoor and outdoor pools, fitness center, and walking distance to the mall. Few residents could afford the rent – most were subsidized by trust funds and parents eager to make life comfortable for their kids. Lindbergh Towers was filled with youthful energy, cheerful indulgence, and an undertow of power seekers. The rollerbladers would one day sit in executive offices beneath golden parachutes; the cyclists on glitzy, thousand dollar bicycles were the name brands of the future. A few meandered in wrinkled green scrubs – medical residents and fellows who would eventually command lucrative practices in their specialties, multiple offices, homes in Garden Village, and yachts docked in Freeport.

Kiran tried to see her condo through Denise Fletcher's eyes – a glistening new kitchen with granite countertops, two bedrooms carefully decorated in soothing colors, a living room painted in sage green, a huge picture window, and a buttery white Italian leather couch. Before she moved in, Kiran had a *feng shui* consultation to make sure that her space was harmonious.

What would Denise Fletcher say about feng shui? Would she approve of her wealthy parents, upscale lifestyle, and handsome lover? A fireman and a social worker? It was a cliché.

Kiran shrugged. It was luck where you were born. Her parents had been desperate to have a baby – they had been married 8 years when Kiran and Robert came along with help from top fertility experts. Their desperation birthed a need to give their twins *everything*. Denise and Al had two grown biological children – one went to college in Queens and the other was a Marine. They became foster parents because they wanted to help needy kids who, in contrast to Kiran, had nothing.

And Joshua? Joshua had less than nothing. He was a beautiful baby with no history. It was easy to fall in love with his poster-child face; harder to connect with him. Joshua was alone, abandoned to the system. What would his life be like if he had been born in Garden Village? What would his life *be* if Kiran and Morgan had been his parents?

There were no answers – there would never be any answers. Yet the questions plagued her, keeping her awake at night and haunting her sleep. Damn. Why did *this* kid get to her? Where are you now, Joshua's Momma?

She took a deep breath. Tomorrow was another day for herself as well as Joshua. She would find another placement. Maybe it would be a foster/adoptive home? Kiran would prepare the foster mom. She glanced at Morgan and knew sleep was not an option. She slipped out of bed and opened her laptop.

Kiran wrote the first of many detailed psychological assessments of Baby Joshua Doe.

He's a beautiful baby boy. He was clean and healthy in the hospital – no indication of prenatal exposure to drugs or alcohol. He spent a week in the hospital because he began to cry and thrash without stopping. The nurses said he was angry. The doctors searched for medical reasons. Nothing was found. One day he stopped. He was quiet.

"He's ready for foster care," the neonatologist announced.

Joshua doesn't like to be held. He's unaffected by other people. He's very calm, as long as he's left alone. He doesn't notice other kids in the home. He doesn't like to suck, so Joshua is a difficult baby to feed. Most of all, Joshua wants to be left untouched, as if he's built a cocoon around himself. This type of behavior can be changed by foster parents who fully understand Joshua's trauma.

Kiran shivered. Can it be changed? What would they have to do?

He needs gentle, patient parents who will make him feel safe. Once he feels safe, Joshua will be the perfect baby. It will take time.

Kiran leaned back, staring at her notes. Would Joshua ever be perfect? Would he ever cuddle or love?

Why Joshua? Why?

There were no answers; only the aggressive glow of her laptop and words that would join the others in Joshua's rapidly swelling file.

Kiran saved everything, and closed the laptop. She mentally went through the list of available families, chasing names like children in a schoolyard. Who would be right for Joshua? Who would know what to do? Somewhere around 3 a.m. she thought of the Candidos. They were the perfect placement for Joshua. They lived in a comfortable house with a spacious backyard. Sharon and Donald couldn't have children. They adopted their first child, Jenny, through an international agency. Jenny, now 6, was Korean-born. Their second daughter, Allyson, was three years old, also adopted through the same international agency. The Candidos wanted a baby boy to complete their family. They registered with DSS.

"We can't afford another international adoption," Sharon had explained.

"We've been so fortunate with the girls," Donald added. "Perhaps we can give a domestic-born baby boy the chance to be part of our family."

Kiran saw a glimmer of hope. She glanced out the window at the setting moon. Partially shielded by clouds, framed by electric wires, the moon glowed as if acknowledging her dilemma. She saw it as an omen.

"Baby Joshua Doe will get another chance," she whispered to the moon.

8

The Candidos lasted 10 months.

"He doesn't like me or any of us," Sharon said tearfully.

"How can a baby not like you?" Kiran asked.

"It's probably me," Sharon hung her head. "I'm used to girls."

"I don't understand."

"He's always angry and withdrawn," Sharon said softly. "He never smiles – he never reaches out to be picked up."

"Maybe he's scared?"

"No," Sharon said sharply. "Babies don't have those kinds of feelings. Joshua is . . . well, he doesn't play any games – no peekaboo or infant games. He doesn't even care when the girls sing."

Kiran blinked.

"Sometimes he sits and bangs his head against the wall. He doesn't cry, he just hits the wall over and over, as if it doesn't hurt him."

"Autistic?"

"No," Sharon said quickly. "No, I don't think he's autistic."

Kiran sighed.

"You have to listen to me," Sharon demanded. "Understand. He's not autistic. He's something . . . else. Joshua is happiest when he's left alone. When no one touches him."

There was a long, tense silence.

"Do you want me to show you?" Sharon asked softly.

Kiran didn't respond.

"Joshua is broken," Sharon whispered, "and I can't help him. He can stay here until you find another placement. We're not adopting him."

Kiran's eyes filled with tears.

Why, Joshua?

9

The world swirls around me.

Faces. Voices. Laughter. Tears.

They come and go without meaning.

She's gone forever. She left me in this chaos. I know. I know why. I'm bad. I'm ugly. She can't bear to see my face. No one can. Everyone waits to throw me away, toss me into a fire of sounds, eyes, and hands that want to touch me. Hold me. Cage me. Her fingers feel like flames burning my skin. Burn. Burn. Burn. A burnt leaf among the dead.

I bang my head against the wall trying to get rid of her. Over and over, harder and harder. Bang. Bang. Bang. It doesn't hurt.

I stay safely within my cocoon. It's the only way. I see no eyes, force no smiles, allow no connect. Within myself, I'm safe. If I allow anyone in, I'll shatter into a thousand pieces. I'll die.

I turn my body away and never let them see, like a broken old toy, burned by the sun. I must survive. I must bang my head harder and harder to survive. That's all I have.

Aldi and Cal

1

Why me?

Aldi held the letter in her hand.

She stared at the words, her eyes blurring with tears. Why always me?

Beth leaped into her mind. Lovely, happy, Beth. Things always went right for *her*. Aldi shook her head angrily. She hated those thoughts. She loved her younger sister, even though Beth was the golden child while she, Aldi, was dark.

Aldi struggled with life. She kept her days simple and inoculated – never playing sports, avoiding music blasted from ear buds, and flat jokes from TV sitcoms. She preferred day dreaming to infatuation with sexy young actors; philosophy over celebrity gossip. Her idols were the romantic heroes of the past – Beowulf and the Lady from Bath; Chaucer and Elizabeth Barrett Browning; the timeless voice of Shakespeare read in a book or thundered from a stage. Classic poetry danced in her head; when she thought of political crisis it was more about The War of the Roses than Democrats battling Republicans across the aisle.

Although people used her childhood nickname, Aldi, she was more like the old Portuguese name that appeared on her birth certificate, *Aldonca*.

"Aldonca is a special name," her mother once explained. "It goes back a long time, to the roots of our family tree. Aldonca was a gentle Christian lady who saved the lives of our ancestors."

Today they called them the *Righteous Among The Nations* – Christians who risked their lives during the Holocaust to save endangered Jews. Names like the Radzio family – Polish Christians who harbored Jews in their home, and Raoul Wallenberg who was credited for saving up to 100,000 Jews in Nazi occupied Hungary filled her head. Perhaps the most famous was Oskar Schindler, a member of the Nazi party who protected 1200 Jews in Krakow, Poland. Aldonca was a righteous hero before there was a name for it.

Aldi didn't particularly like being named for a righteous hero. It felt like she had a responsibility – a legacy to maintain – forced to live up to something she wasn't.

"It fits," her mother, Espie, said. "In a strange way, it fits perfectly. Names always do."

Everyone, including her parents, thought she was strange.

"You're an anachronism," Espie added, believing it was a compliment. It was an excuse and they both knew it. Aldi never quite fit in anywhere, except among thinkers, philosophers, and those buried in intellectual delusion. A psychology professor called her an *outlier* – someone who functioned outside the bell curve of normalcy.

Aldi shuddered.

An outlier.

It sounded like a curse – the same as her name. Aldi lived with expectations where she always fell short; failure as a way of life. The pressure was never really understood – even as an adolescent, Aldi confused her family. When Beth became a teenager, her parents were thrilled. Finally they had a pretty, partying, people-loving *normal* kid. Aldi was jealous, but Beth was someone she could never emulate. The fierce escapades of Henry VIII and the "favorite wife," Ann Boleyn, captured Aldi's imagination – they were far more fascinating than who got invited to the prom or the dress worn by the homecoming queen. Beth made lots of mistakes, but was always forgiven for being young and impulsive. Beth had boyfriends, lovers, and dramatic breakups. Aldi only had one, and no one ever knew.

Aldi took a deep breath and raised the paper, her hand shaking. She read the first line of the letter and shuddered.

Thank you for giving us this opportunity to introduce ourselves.

Aldi groaned.

Why me? Who would ever want us?

Beth, with her charming smile, drew everyone's attention. Beth could dance like a professional and bring a grin to the most unrelenting face. Not surprisingly, Beth married Thomas, a successful corporate VP, on his ascent to the top, and produced two beautiful girls, appropriately named Sage and Danielle. Danielle looked like her parents while Sage had the dark skin, red hair, and hazel eyes of her Grandma Espie. The girls had "gifted" pinned to their baby blankets, growing up gracefully while their mother pursued an exquisitely feminine career as a pre-k teacher.

"It's a great career," Beth had explained when she was 18 years old, long before she met Thomas. They were in Beth's pink bedroom, filled with photos, cards, and paper hearts. Beth was going out; Aldi was staying in. Aldi watched her little sister dab bright red lipstick, dark mascara, and prohibitively expensive blush. Beth batted her eyes. "I'll have it all."

Having it all was unimaginable to Aldi.

"Sure," Beth predicted. "I'll have it all – a husband who makes lots of money, good sex, a cleaning lady, expensive clothes, *and* a career. You know, work, tennis, and supermom?" Beth laughed, a sound that reminded Aldi of Christmas and the tinkle of brightly painted red metal bells.

A cliché, Aldi thought. Beth was always a cliché, like a romance novel with life mapped skillfully within chapters and predictable plots.

Not like me.

Aldi was chubby, intense, hated parties, sported impossible hair, and was more comfortable around books than people. Her idea of a good time was sitting with a few colleagues, sipping wine and munching cheese with odd names like *Aged Manchego*, *Wensleydale*, and *Drunken Goat;* conversation centered on the hapless human condition. She loved the heady intensity of cerebral debate, wandering into places that bored most people; sharing theories and ideas that few ever considered. They were Aldi's happiest moments – immersed in collaborative thought that expanded her well-informed imagination. Aldi's throat constricted. She thought fondly of those times with fellow outliers.

"Your friends are boring," Beth dismissed Aldi's world. "Who cares?"

"I care."

Beth shrugged. "When do you have fun?"

There was a better question.

When is it my turn?

2

Aldi battled anger, then grief, like a soldier in a foxhole. Beth's life was a construct Aldi could never embrace. Her mother's promise drifted in her head.

"Your time will come, dear. I just know it."

The voice wasn't convincing. If Aldi's time was going to come, why did she have to write this letter? Why did she have to undergo 5 years of gut-wrenching doubt, and heartbreak, month after month, on a dream that would never be realized? In her soul, Aldi knew the truth.

I'm being punished.

For the first and only time I tried to be like Beth.

Aldi shook off the thought. It was an assault of retribution – her superego punishing her for an act nearly a decade old. Her life felt like a morality play – payback for betrayal.

Aldi returned to the paper in her hand. Thoughts of Beth made no sense. Aldi would never be her sister; would never be able to think or behave like her. Aldi cleared her throat, squared her shoulders, and forced herself to reread the first awful words in the letter.

Thank you for giving us this opportunity to introduce ourselves.

When would someone thank Aldi for not hating Beth? Thank her for being a loyal sister and dutiful aunt? For keeping her pain silent, tucked inside, so no one would see? For never telling *anyone*, particularly Cal, the truth?

"It's all very simple," her mother had said. "You are who you are. It is what it is."

Aldi wanted to scream. They were such nonsensical words. Yet they carried a poignant, timeless truth. She wanted to toss the words in the air and shoot them with a burst of fire from a 17th century flintlock pistol.

Don't you get it Mother? I deserve this.

Aldi languished in a self-imposed inquisition cell watching dreams play out in other people's lives.

Aldi took a deep breath that felt more like a wheeze. She reviewed the words that spelled out her life on one ridiculous page.

It was a DBM – Dear Birth Mother letter – a marketing concept in the world of open adoption. The premise was simple. There were Birth Mothers, or pregnant women looking to give up their babies for adoption. They contacted agencies, adoption attorneys, answered classified ads, or searched the internet to find suitable parents for their unborn children. They reviewed stacks of DBM letters that introduced couples looking to adopt children. Using these marketing tools, Birth Mothers narrowed their choices to select a lucky couple. The problem was that there were far too many infertile couples vying to snag a Birth Mother. The number grew constantly; the competition more intense. The adopting couples had been screened by agencies and attorneys, endured extensive home studies, supplied mountains of paperwork, a photo portfolio, and attended special classes to demonstrate that they exceeded all the selection criteria. They were all good choices; all ready to grow their families; and all desperate to adopt a child. How could one stand out above the others?

What a system, Aldi thought. Buying into the fragile, hormone-infused minds of young girls dealing with unwanted pregnancies.

She shuddered. Right now it was their only alternative. Their adoption attorney, William Chain III, was a God, in his dark, high-backed leather chair in a wood paneled office filled with law tomes and photos of "happy American families." Wearing a plastic smile, he painted a very clear picture.

"Sell yourselves," William Chain III declared, as if he were stating his retainer. "Look good. That's all these Birth Mothers want." He stared impassively at Aldi and Cal.

Look good?

"Birth Mothers," he continued, "want to know that their babies will be raised in the families of their dreams – not like the families where they grew up. You have to appear like a fantasy-come-true, while sticking to the facts. Do you understand?"

Aldi winced. How does one look good after years of devastating infertility treatments, known euphemistically as *ART* – Assistive Reproduction Technology? How do you swallow the emotional crashes; tuck away feelings that you're inferior to a high school dropout because she pushes a stroller? How do you leapfrog the deep, pervasive sense of loss that permeates you, your marriage, and your parents' silent disappointment?

Aldi's parents *tried* to help, but they *always* talked about grandchildren. Through all the treatment and agonizing waits, they asked painful questions and made offers.

"If it's a money problem, we'll help you."

"Your mother would *love* more grandchildren. When will it happen?"

"Just *relax* and it will happen when you least expect it."

They never guessed it was about Aldi and her treachery. Infertility was her sentence.

How do I live with my betrayal, Mother? How do I accept my punishment, Father?

They never heard the questions or knew the answers. They never even guessed. Aldi kept it all tucked neatly inside – a secret that gave birth to self-flagellation.

Chain introduced another dimension.

"It's really quite simple," Chain observed. "Follow the rules."

Aldi sighed. So few understood the struggle; the heart wrenching pain that didn't even play out well in prime time TV. *Infertility* – the ugliest word in the language.

Aldi took a deep breath. She and Cal had supposedly "moved on." After ART failure, there was adoption with its wild kingdom of reprehensible choices – open, agency, attorney, trans-racial, international, domestic, foster . . . negotiating it was daunting. Each step came with endless paperwork and costs, further chipping away from savings drained by ART. Enter William Chain III, who summed them up in dollar bills. His words were as soothing as the needle sticks in infertility treatment.

Aldi lost hope. Nothing seemed to work. So when William Chain III collected his down payment and told them to write a DBM letter, she and Cal numbly complied. Now, with a DBM and their best photo, there was nothing else to pursue.

I'm sorry Mother, Father. I'm sorry I failed you, too.

Aldi shook away the thoughts. Look at us. Aldi held the photo up to the light. I'm short and round; my hair is too brown and my eyes are too small; I look like a childless nursery school teacher ready to kidnap the next kid that walks into the playhouse. And Cal? He was worse, with his chubby face, double chin, thick round wire glasses, and smile that said "I hate this stuff." Who would ever choose them? Even more revealing, they looked inconsolable.

Please, pul-lease like me.

Please, pul-lease give us your baby.

If I were a Birth Mother, Aldi thought, I would look for a slim couple, who loved to climb mountains and eat health food. I would want pretty faces that grinned pleasantly in photos and religiously attended baseball games, block parties, and oversized family reunions. People of faith, who attended services every Sunday and baked for the annual church picnic.

That's where Beth failed, too. Aldi and her family were Sephardic Jews with a history of discrimination and expulsion that could be traced back to 15th century Spain. They were haunted by their family tree. Sometimes, Aldi felt more comfortable imagining herself in the dark alleys and narrow steps of medieval Spain than on Sunrise Highway, along the Long Island Railroad tracks, or in her cozy Long Island home.

3

It took Aldi and Cal three weeks to write the letter – checking every DBM book on the shelf and online, and hundreds of websites. They discussed the issues endlessly, worrying like two overwrought investors in a tumbling stock market. When they were finished, Aldi edited out all the scholarly references, convoluted psychology, and awkward academic paradigms that were part of their daily language.

"You think too much," Aldi admonished Cal, knowing she shared the same problem. "We have to dumb it down."

Cal had no idea what she was talking about.

"Analysis paralysis," Aldi said flippantly. "Let's face it; most people don't have our IQs. Most people don't think or talk like us. They want sit coms and *McDonalds*, not Shakespeare and brie."

Cal shrugged. "Whatever you think is best."

"We're outliers," Aldi mumbled.

"Is that so bad?"

Aldi grimaced and thought of Chain. "We have to make our DBM as simple, honest, and direct as possible. Like talking to a four year old."

It didn't work. If the letter didn't bore the Birth Mother, one look at the photo and she would quickly reject the image. After all, how many PhD candidates were looking for parents to adopt their babies?

Aldi shook her head and reread the DBM for the 20th time.

She could hear Chain's voice. "Fill your DBM with teddy bears, snuggles, and an outdoor lifestyle. Be cute and cuddly – the ideal American couple who loves family picnics and biking trips. This is a sales letter – make sure the Birth Mother wants you."

Aldi wondered if his idea of soft was a wad of hundred dollar bills.

Cal was oblivious. "No problem."

It was a problem. Neither of them fit the mold and the best DBM couldn't hide the facts. They wrote and rewrote the letter until they were surrounded by crumpled balls of fine, white watermarked stationary.

4

Dear Birth Mother.

Thank you for giving us this opportunity to introduce ourselves. We are Aldi and Cal. We are very grateful that you love your unborn child so much that you're considering adoption. If you choose us, we will provide a warm home, stimulating intellectual environment, and loving family for your baby.

The story of our marriage is a tale of true love, as written by so many of the great poets of the world. We met 9 years ago on a blind date – introduced by my younger sister, Beth, who now has 2 children in a gifted program. We were so fortunate to have found each other! We are still in awe that we hadn't met earlier. As soul mates, it was romantic love at first sight!

We have always wanted to be parents. When nature didn't bless us with a baby, we submitted to 5 fruitless years of infertility treatments (drugs, tests, insemination, in vitro). We exhausted our physical and emotional resources, burying the hope that our bodies would bring forth children. Putting biology to rest, we decided to pursue our dreams of a family in another way – adoption.

Adoption is the perfect alternative for us. We want to nurture our family and raise our children in a rich atmosphere of joy, togetherness, and intellectual pursuit.

We live in a large, warm Gothic house, built in brick with white trim, in Smithville, Long Island. We're walking distance to Walden Pond – a lovely fishing pond and park that was used by the Merokee Indians, before the settlers came from New Amsterdam in the 17th century. It's a great place to hike, commune with nature, or go fishing.

Sometimes we follow one of the trails around the pond, sit on a flat rock, discuss transcendentalism, and watch the Canadian Geese. We talk about how God has blessed us with so much – except a baby!

Aldi comes from a loving family who lives nearby in North Smithville. She has one sister (the one who introduced us) who is three years younger. Beth is married to Thomas, a prominent corporate executive. They have two beautiful little girls, Sage and Danielle, and live one town away in Merokee Harbor. We spend a lot of time together. Aldi's parents, Espie and Eli, can't wait to become grandparents again.

Aldi works as an administrator in the University's School of Education, evaluating text books, the latest theories on education, and teaching undergraduate courses in the philosophy of education. She holds a doctorate in Education.

In her spare time, Aldi takes out her favorite *Forged Premio* chef's knife and cooks a fabulous meal. She's a great chef! Her signature dish is a Portuguese-inspired ground beef, sliced mushrooms, chopped tomatoes, and gravy made with a splash of *Vinho do Porto*. When our child arrives, Aldi will be a stay-at-home mom and teach only at night when Cal watches the baby.

Cal owns an antiquarian and rare books store called the *Tree of Life*. He sells fine collectible books. Cal holds a PhD in world history, and is very well respected in his field. His exclusive store sits on *Poet's Corner*, a local historic shopping district a few minutes from the house. Since the store is so close to home, Cal will help Aldi, go to school conferences, and cheer our child in whatever activities he or she chooses. Cal wants to be the best father in the world – especially since his parents and younger brother passed away in a tragic car accident a few years ago.

In his spare time, Cal tinkers in his woodworking shop located at the rear of our house. He builds small, desktop bookcases in the classic Roycroft style, with exotic woods like acacia – the wood used for the *Ark of the Covenant* in the Bible.

Thank you for taking the time to read about us. We are good, nurturing, generous, and supportive people who would give your child unconditional love, happiness, and security. You will have peace of mind that your baby is being raised in a gentle and intellectually stimulating environment. Please contact us!

Sincerely,
Aldi and Cal

5

Aldi felt nauseous. She rubbed her barren belly, took a deep breath, and called Cal on his cell.

"I think it's done," she said softly.

"Good, send it out." His voice was curt – she knew there had to be a customer nearby.

"I can't. It's pitiful."

"Aldi, I can't talk right now . . ."

"What if it doesn't work? This is our last chance . . ." Tears trickled down her face.

"You have to. It's our only option," Cal softened his voice.

"No one will like us."

"There's someone waiting for us out there . . ."

Aldi wiped her tears angrily.

"OK," Cal sighed. "I'm sorry – I know how you feel." He paused. Then he gave the directive that would change their lives forever. "Go to Chain's office and hand deliver the DBM. It'll make you feel better."

Aldi stopped crying.

"I have to go now," Cal said gently. He broke the connect.

Aldi stared at the phone for a long time. It was dead, like so many of her fantasies. Dead, like the dreams she had about a swollen pregnant belly, giving birth in a midwife center, and cradling her newborn when it was minutes old. Dead like her dreams of creating life seeded from her and Cal; children that would carry their genes.

Dead like the other baby.

She fought the memories but they flooded her mind, beyond her mental control. The last five years and their excruciating ordeal refused to be ignored. Watching Beth with her children fueled Aldi's need to have a baby, and at the same time, heightened her failure. Often it hovered on the edge of obsession.

I need a child that belongs to me.

In the beginning, they had so much hope. It was just a matter of tossing the birth control pills in the trash. Pregnancy seemed like a natural progression; an entitlement. Month after month she bled; the red stains signaling her failure. It became unbearable as she watched new children cycle into the neighborhood as if there was another baby, new parents, and happy families *every day*. The months bled into two years and Aldi knew she had to move on to the dreaded ARTs – assisted reproduction technologies. The acronym made her wince; Aldi loved the warm, graceful past and like Cal, was afraid of the stainless steel world of technology.

"It will happen," her mother assured Aldi. "You need patience and time. Relax."

Aldi hated that word. *Relax*. But it wasn't until her mother said off-handedly, "maybe you should go to *someone*," that Aldi took the leap.

Their internist, a gentle man in his 60s, referred them to an infertility specialist. Even now, after all this time, the word *infertility* made her shiver like it was a death sentence. At first, it was some simple tests. Then the tests got more complicated and more invasive. Before she knew it, Aldi was on drugs that made her angry and aggressive; descriptors that had never been a part of who she was. She failed a lot of her students that semester, slashing their papers with angry red marks. The needles were next; the fantastically expensive in vitro; and the mind-numbing failures. Frustrated, they priced out surrogates only to decide that going outside the country wasn't an option. Their heads were spinning. They discovered that the chances of successful ART were pitifully low, something they never quite realized. After five years, they came home one day and stared at each other.

We're done.

Now, here they were with a DBM begging a faceless young woman for her baby. Aldi felt like a dying leaf, floating in a bottomless puddle of black water.

6

William Chain III was behind a closed door, convincing a new couple that adoption was their only solution. Aldi stared at his secretary. She was ten years younger, sporting long blonde hair stained with black highlights. Her claw-like red nails looked as if they came out of a horror magazine.

"I'm sorry he can't see you," Jaime, the secretary, said in response to her request. "You know how these things work. You need to make an appointment."

Aldi nodded. It had made no sense to take Cal's suggestion and hand deliver the DBM. Standing in William Chain III's office didn't make her feel any better. It was an impulsive move, possibly the result of a useless school holiday. Strange coincidences happened on those days when there was too much time.

"I shouldn't have come," Aldi said slowly, her cheeks reddening. "I just . . ."

Jaime's eyes filled with sympathy. She glanced at the paper in Aldi's hands. "I can take that and put it on his desk when he's finished."

Aldi nodded. "Thank you."

"DBM?" Jaime asked softly.

Suddenly, the secretary's brown eyes captured Aldi, as if she knew something more; an insider's secret. Aldi frowned.

What was there left to know?

Barren. Aldi thought of the old-fashioned word used to describe infertility. She was a barren, childless woman.

"Yes," Aldi grimaced. "Our DBM."

Jaime shook her head wisely. "Those are so awful to write – I feel sorry for couples like you."

Aldi was silent. She didn't need sympathy. She needed a baby.

"There is hope, " Jaime smiled. "Many of our parents built their families . . ."

Aldi cut her off. "Not for us. Who would want *us* to be their baby's parents?"

"Don't think like that."

Aldi shook her head. "We don't climb mountains and snack on granola bars. We're fat, ugly, and desperate. We don't even go to church."

"No!" Jaime said sharply. "You're good people."

Aldi smiled sadly. "Here," she handed Jaime the DBM. Jaime read it quickly. Aldi saw, by the expression on her face, that it was not going to convince anyone. The letter was as awkward as they were – outliers in a conventional world.

"Good job," Jaime said weakly. "I'll give it to him as soon as he's finished."

Aldi shrugged. "I think," she whispered, "that there are no children in our future." Her eyes filled with tears.

"No," Jaime grabbed her hand.

Aldi pulled her hand away and wiped her eyes impatiently. "Thank you," she moved back.

"Wait. Have you ever considered foster care? There are people who give up babies – toddlers – who have nowhere to go. Foster parents often take in kids who they adopt. It's another way to . . ."

Aldi stared at her.

"Listen," Jaime continued. "You can't say anything to him," she tilted her head towards William Chain's closed office door. "It's bad for business." She smiled weakly and spoke in a whisper.

Aldi lowered her eyes.

"My boyfriend Hector is a fireman. His partner is this guy, Morgan, whose girlfriend is a social worker with DSS. Kind of complicated, huh? Well her name is Kiran. Maybe she can help." Jaime scrawled a number on a sticky note. "Maybe she knows someone."

"Maybe," Aldi conceded. "Thank you." She reluctantly took the sticky note and headed home.

Later, Aldi crumpled the note and buried it in her kitchen desk drawer.

She waited two months. There was no response to the DBM.

Aldi knew that nothing would happen. It was as if God, karma, or some unknown cosmic force was punishing her for that night, when she was barely 26, and made a decision that would haunt her for the rest of her life.

"It doesn't hurt to call DSS," Aldi finally said to Cal.

Perhaps taking someone else's broken child was what she was meant to do?

He shrugged. Cal was waiting for the shipment of a small estate library, making a mental list of how he would catalogue and price the titles. "I'm not sure that's what we want," he mumbled.

"What?"

"A foster child." Cal said firmly. "There's no way of knowing what you get."

Aldi nodded. "We won't know the family tree but if we love him – protect him from any more hurt – we'll show him that the world can be a good place."

"That's not easy. We don't even *know* what we're talking about. You and I – we know a lot about history, literature, and philosophy. But children?"

"I'm an educator."

"An educator at the university is very different than a parent at home."

"How can you say that?"

"You teach theories not childcare."

Aldi took a deep breath.

"Maybe we can get a foster *baby*. A child without baggage who isn't old enough to experience trauma . . ."

"Tabula rasa?"

"Yes."

"And genes? Don't they play a part?"

"Gene sequences are triggered by the environment."

"No one is sure."

"That's exactly my point." Aldi grinned. "We can work with it. Not ignore the problems. Get help if it's needed. It's not that difficult."

Cal was silent.

"Come on," she added sweetly. "Think about it this way – Nelson Mandela, Eriq LaSalle, and Babe Ruth were all foster kids."

"Nelson Mandela?"

"Yes."

"You have a point there."

Cal conceded. It was easier than arguing.

Aldi's parents and Beth were not as easy to convince. They mirrored Cal's objections.

"A *foster* child?" Beth said, sounding shocked.

"You never know?" Mother was uncertain. "I mean, a foster child could come with all sorts of problems."

In the end, Aldi convinced them all.

Like Cal, it was a lot easier to agree than to argue.

Aldi switched gears. She composed an image of a lost little boy in her mind – complete with a dirty, oversized knapsack, trapped behind a grungy metal fence, and leaning against a stained concrete wall. He was looking for a forever home.

Aldi would save him.

7

Cal returned to his routine.

As Aldi resigned herself to make The Call, she could no longer fight off the nightmare that ran through her head like a Shakespearean tragedy. The scenes repeated themselves in instant replays; the drama a permanent part of who she had become. Sometimes, Aldi cherished the secret; she loved the idea of having knowledge that no one shared. Most of the time, she kept it buried, horrified, fighting to forget. But she never forgot; it became part of her life, consciously and unconsciously, driving choices she never quite grasped.

A tragic flaw.

Now it came back, crashing her defences; carrying visions that excited and terrified her; shock waves that made her dizzy, weak, and angry.

Aldi was only 26 years old and a newlywed when it happened. She loved Cal and his charming, old-fashioned ways. He relished the past while living grudgingly in the present. His storehouse of information crossed the millennium; his photographic memory noting each fact. Their wedding had been small, in an old mansion in the country. Their honeymoon was devoted to exploring the art, ruins, and architecture in Europe. They spent the entire summer session away from home and the university, releasing the past, along with the passion in their bodies. It had been idyllic.

Aldi remembered that summer as the best in her life. For once, she felt better to be herself than Beth. She and Cal explored the ruins in Rome and gazed unabashedly at the Vatican and Sistine Chapel. They plunged into a romantic past, touching castles and caves, gawking at art venerated in textbooks, and architecture they had seen only on glossy plates in coffee table books and art history texts. They held hands as they walked *Las Ramblas* in Barcelona, laughing at the living statues and inhaling heady scents from kiosks bursting with flowers. They stood in awe of medieval Girona where Kabbalists like Nachmonides once thrived. They clamored across the ramparts of *Castelo de São Jorge* and paused to take in the view of Lisbon and the Tagus River, talking about the kids who were kidnapped and shipped to *São Tomé*.

They laughed and called one another their real names, both of Portuguese origin.

"Aldonca, my love," Cal whispered as he kissed her neck.

"Goncallo, my knight," Aldi giggled.

In London, they saw the Tower and Crown Jewels; visited the poet's corner in Westminster Abbey, awed by the monuments to Geoffrey Chaucer and William Shakespeare. They were intimate with history and each other, making love with an intensity neither had ever experienced.

"You're beautiful," Cal said, over and over.

Aldi wondered what he saw, but relished his words.

I'm not Beth and he loves me.

"I love you more than life itself," he whispered in the narrow beds of the tiny *pensiones* where they slept.

That summer, Aldi and Cal owned the world and each other.

"You're both anachronisms," Aldi's mother observed when they returned home. "A match made in heaven." She said it affectionately, understanding the wonder that pervaded the newlyweds. Espie looked at their travel photos, listened to their stories, and knew that her curious daughter was happy.

It *was* a perfect romance and Aldi was happier than she had ever thought possible. Even Beth told Aldi that she looked beautiful.

At the end of the summer, Aldi and Cal returned to campus. The honeymoon stretched into their new apartment, brazen and unrestrained; life with endless possibilities.

Until that day.

Life crashed.

Two policemen knocked politely on the door. It was 9 p.m. Aldi would never forget that moment. She opened the door and they asked for Cal. She didn't question them, but stood by, close to her new husband. They told him there had been an accident; a DWI, his parents, and brother were dead.

Cal smiled. "It can't be them," he said pleasantly. "They don't drink."

The police were gentle. "Can we come in?"

Cal stood aside. "Of course, but you're making a mistake."

They reviewed what had happened.

Driving on the Long Island Expressway. A DWI crossed the divider and hit them head on. There was no chance anyone could survive. Fire and explosions. Twisted metal. Even the DWI died.

"No," Cal insisted. "You don't understand."

They waited patiently, as he called their landline. They waited patiently as he called their cell phones. All three. Mother. Father. Edmund.

No answer.

Cal turned to look at them. His smile was gone.

We're so sorry, they said. So sorry.

Tears streamed down Aldi's face.

"Why are you crying, Aldi. Why?"

She held him but Cal refused to believe the story.

"Don't you understand, Aldi? In all due respect, officers, this is a very big mistake."

They took him to the morgue. There were enough remains to identify the charred, dead faces of his family.

Cal collapsed.

He fell into a deep depression, clinging to Aldi as if she were his only hope. The summer faded into months of pain; the funeral, the shiva, and the clearing away of three lives. Cal agonized over every piece, clinging to the smallest keepsakes, cluttering their apartment with unfamiliar stuff. Aldi stood by faithfully, through the estate settlement, preparing and selling the house, struggling with Cal's grief. She never left his side.

By the spring semester, Aldi was exhausted.

I want to be happy again.

Life around them moved on. The seasons changed; there were new students and new classes; new headlines and new books. Cal remained crushed – a shell of his former self. He didn't smile or tell Aldi he loved her. He didn't say she was beautiful. He clung, lifeless, to her.

I want more.

I love him but I want more. I want the summer back.

Aldi couldn't tell Cal any of that. She knew that grief was like a wound to the body – it took a long time to heal. It was simply too soon to expect recovery. Yet Aldi was tired of being sad; tired of being cold and untouched. She had a taste of Beth-style happiness, and couldn't go back.

8

It was a lifetime ago.

Aldi couldn't handle Cal's grief. It was as if the world had permanently turned grey. Until *he* arrived on campus.

The School of Education was angry about school cutbacks, teacher layoffs, and a barrage of tests that transformed the art of teaching into probabilities and percentages. The concept of teacher accountability had been twisted into an excuse to foster mediocrity. Students and professors were restless. It had moved beyond complaints into a fervent demand for change. Protests were organized and signs made from old pieces of painted wood with the mantra scrawled in black.

The voices rose in unison.

Teach Washington now. Teach Washington how schools work. Teach Washington what children need. Teach Washington that teachers can make it happen.

Teach Washington How!

Teach Washington How!

It was a grassroots call to action with remnants of 60s protestors. Everyone was eager to bring back the bad old days. Politicians immediately recognized the new movement as a means to expand the voter base. Local legislators greedily climbed aboard the bandwagon. The Senator joined them, claiming to be a leader of students and educators fighting for a better future. It was basic political sport – *he* became their voice in Washington.

There were rumors about his taste for adolescent girls, but who cared when his voice was strong, he looked sincere, and his charisma was pervasive? His constituency forgave him. No one was perfect. When he spoke at the university, people were awed by his eloquence and unquestioning loyalty to their cause: family values and education. He coined a new tagline and human rights agency: *Family Reigns Supreme.*

In the beginning, Aldi was aloof.

"Join us," her Department Chair suggested. "You'll get involved in something beyond your own troubles, have your voice heard. Get out; risk being outside your own skin."

The implication was clear. Aldi should put distance between herself and Cal's grief. It wasn't her style, but she was lost and in desperate need for respite.

"I'll try," Aldi agreed unhappily

She began quietly, as a spectator, and was drawn into the crowd, her voice rising with the collective chant.

Teach Washington How!

Teach Washington How!

Aldi ventured beyond the walls of the university and her marriage. She attended Town Hall events and community demonstrations. Aldi could breathe easier when she immersed herself there. She had never experienced so many people who thrived in the present, demanding change in the illusion of a rosy future. It was a stark contrast to attorneys, estate settlements, and her husband's raw depression. For the first and only time in her life, Aldi felt she could have an impact on the world.

The Senator's campaign staff recognized Aldi's potential as a local asset, playing a natural role in winning new young voters. A University School of Education administrator would give authenticity to his platform. Aldi was young, intelligent, educated, and loaded with credentials. She wasn't beautiful, but that was an advantage with his shaky sexual reputation. Clearly, her age and position was a notch on his political belt.

So Aldi became a part of something larger than herself. It felt comfortable and right; a compromise between her and the rest of the world, as if she had drifted invisibly into a foreign domain.

Cal kept his distance. He wasn't interested in contemporary politics or reform; only sinking deeper into the strategies of renaissance European royalty. He focused on the macabre – royal conspiracies, ancient assassinations, and historical genocides.

"You must understand," Cal said cryptically, "history repeats itself. We're only going to change if we integrate the lesson of yesterday into today." He sighed. "Something *no one* has been able to do."

Aldi heard it in his voice.

No hope.

She was too young to give up. "It's been a horrible time, but you have to think *today* for a change."

"Today?" Cal's eyes were wide and angry. "There's no today."

She knew it was grief speaking; eventually Cal would recover; but it was taking too long.

"The spiritualists say there's *only* today. The past is over and the future doesn't yet exist."

She quoted the novelist, J.B. Priestly.

Today is the tomorrow you worried about yesterday.

"Don't be an idiot." Cal's eyes filled with disdain.

Aldi was furious. Cal sounded like an old man – a suffocating anachronism.

"People," Cal snarled, not noticing her reaction. "People have to make a serious commitment not to repeat the errors of humankind that have persisted since the beginning of civilization."

Aldi tuned him out, like switching off the TV. She shifted her attention, knowing he was still struggling to make sense of his losses. Aldi was determined not to let Cal stop her; she refused to remain in his angry, depressed bed. She embraced the cause. Community leaders, local and national politicians, and activists suddenly cycled through her office before making appearances in university lecture halls and meetings. The activity was dizzying; Cal watched and listened with skepticism.

"Don't get your hopes up," Cal advised. "Teach Washington How! is just a collection of sound bites."

She didn't listen. Aldi felt alive.

Maybe Cal will feel me slipping away and wake up?

The political aides increasingly drew Aldi into the fray. She became the voice that local students and their parents trusted. She welcomed them into her new world of optimistic educators who believed in change. Everyone loved her.

One day she was invited to meet The Senator. Aldi trembled as she shook his hand, as if in the presence of greatness. The second time it was easier, ignoring the sweat that trickled down the small of her back.

"Don't be afraid of me child," he whispered in her ear. "We're on the same side."

Aldi smiled nervously.

"You're Espie's daughter?" He asked casually.

"Yes. Do you know her?"

"From a long time ago." An edge crept into his voice.

Aldi stared at him, curious. "Where?"

His eyes seized hers. Aldi couldn't speak. Instinctively, she knew to remain quiet. She didn't want to know what had gone on between The Senator and her mother.

"Teach Washington How," Aldi said weakly.

A smile curled his lips but never entered his eyes.

"Teach Washington How!" he echoed, patting her arm.

Aldi felt dizzy; a teenage groupie screaming for her rock star; willing to do almost anything for attention from her idol.

"I don't know what you see in the man," Cal later pontificated. "He's an aging Shylock looking for votes."

Aldi was horrified. Cal was completely out of touch. He had no clue about the campaign and its goal.

No clue.

9

Aldi started staying late in her university office. There were increasing piles of work for *Teach Washington Now!* She put in extra hours to do her daily work and to keep up with the campaign. When she worked nights, Aldi tied up her hair, lingered in the silent building, and gazed dreamily at her computer. By the time she got home, Cal was asleep. She didn't have to face his depression.

Aldi discovered it was pleasant to work in an empty, quiet space, planning an optimistic future. The brick building was empty and the lights dim except for her office. It was an odd thrill to be so *alone*. Her head was filled with change. She wanted to scream so everyone could hear.

I'm alive.

I'm not dead like his family.

The cries were in her head, and Aldi let them settle, edging her through the dark hours at home.

One night, a silhouette appeared in her doorway. Aldi looked up and caught her breath. It was The Senator. He was fiercely good-looking in the dim light; tall, with a deep voice, composed smile, and hypnotic eyes. He moved in aristocratic grace, tossing his thinning, caramel-colored hair as he held his head high, squared his shoulders, and spoke in an arrogant, compelling voice. Although he was 27 years older than Aldi, he seemed younger than Cal. He came into her office and closed the door behind him.

"Teach Washington How," he said as a greeting.

She smiled nervously as he approached her.

"Aldi," he said intimately.

Aldi never knew that her old name could sound erotic.

"Aldi," he repeated, and went to her desk.

She couldn't take her eyes off him; her heart pounded; and she couldn't speak. The months of grieving and depression shifted, replaced by his face.

"Aldi," he said, and gently edged her chair away from the desk. He touched her hair, running his fingers down her neck. "Aldi," he said thickly, "I want you."

She was stunned. He paused politely, as if waiting for permission.

"I'm married," she whispered, but he ignored her.

"You're beautiful," he said, bending to kiss her neck. "So young. Such intensity."

Aldi's heart pounded wildly; she didn't know what to do – what to say. He was such an important man and he wanted her . . .

"I'm married," she repeated softly.

His fingers curled beneath her blouse, expertly snapping open her bra. Aldi shivered. She didn't stop him. She knew it was wrong; she should back off before it was too late. How could she betray Cal when he was so vulnerable?

I need to feel good again.

He spoke in soft, soothing tones as his fingers explored her breasts. He pressed his mouth against her ear, his voice thick with desire.

"Aldi," he caressed her name. "I've wanted you since the first moment I saw you. Your beauty outside only matches your beauty inside – you make me dizzy with desire. I dream about holding your body, naked, against me. Making love . . ."

It had been so long.

Although he sounded like a cheap romance novel; although she knew it wasn't true, Aldi wanted to be seduced. She wanted to feel like Beth again – pretty, loved, and admired.

I want my happy back.

"Aldi, my love," he explored her ear with his tongue. "So young. So sweet."

What would it be like to do something utterly, wildly wrong?

He buried his face in her breasts. Then he took each breast in his mouth, his tongue sending electric shocks through her body, carrying her to a place she never knew existed. He toyed with her nipples until they were hard and wildly sensitized. He guided her off the chair and onto the floor, expertly sliding off her skirt and panties, tracing every part of her body with his fingers and tongue. Aldi climaxed again and again, reaching dizzying heights that Cal never approached. Then he slipped off his pants and plunged into her. Fiery colors burst behind her closed eyelids; her body throbbed with each thrust.

When it was over, he left her sprawled and dazed on the floor.

He got dressed, straightened his clothes, and looked down at her on the floor. "Tomorrow Aldi? Same time?"

She knew it was wrong. She knew she had betrayed Cal. She stared into The Senator's blue eyes and couldn't speak.

Aldi couldn't refuse him.

He smiled. The most beautiful smile in the world. "Thank you. Thank you. Thank you." He said smoothly.

He came every other weekday for a month. It was a tight, skillfully devised schedule. She did whatever he wanted. The days and weekends were excuses – time passed for the nights. Aldi had never felt so weak and controlled – so powerful and fulfilled – at the same time.

Sometimes he got rough.

The Senator would plunge into her, without foreplay, hissing into her ear. "I'm going to fuck you kike, like you've never been fucked before."

He twisted her arms and bit her breasts, grabbed her wrists, and pounded her body. She was scared; it hurt and was crazy exciting at the same time. Other times he would thrust his penis into her mouth, leaving a sticky trail on her tongue.

Aldi screamed and cried. She was hungry and fevered, lost in his grasp.

He left for Washington, D.C. under a sky pulsating with the same colors she saw when he made love to her – except now there were black clouds within the fire.

10

Aldi needed to erase The Senator and his fire. It was too late. The two fused together, embedded in her mind like a Shakespearean tragedy that couldn't be edited.

Aldi knew she was pregnant before she took the test.

She was angry at herself for not insisting on condoms or restarting her stash of birth control pills. She could only hear his voice, telling her he loved it that way. Skin-to-skin, nothing coming between their passion.

"I believed," she said out loud to no one. "I believed."

It didn't matter. The Senator was back in Washington and out of her life. He didn't call, and when Aldi tried to contact him, his aides blocked access. Aldi knew what their affair was – a sexual indulgence that would have to be kept buried inside her for the rest of her life.

A quick fuck for The Senator – and me.

What about Cal? He was still depressed. Maybe she could deceive him – convince Cal that the baby was his. How? Cal was still mourning. They hadn't had sex since the day the policemen arrived at their door. Cal was still immersed in grief and survivor's guilt. She wondered if she could deceive him, but the man was too smart. The word popped into her head. *Cuckold.* It was an old term for a married man whose wife cheated on him. They used to giggle over the sound, analyzing Iago's famous words in Shakespeare's *Othello.*

. . . That cuckold lives in bliss,
Who certain of his fate, loves not his wronger:

Aldi thought of Kathryn Howard, Henry VIII's fifth wife who was 30 years younger than her husband – the king's "rose without a thorn." Howard was beheaded for adultery. There were so many others, like Madame Bovary, Cleopatra, and Hester Prynne. Cal would know all of them. He would thrust Aldi into a different group, far from being a "rose without a thorn." She would be just like the others. Aldi had betrayed him during the worst time in his life; embracing a man who was just looking for a . . . quick fuck.

What kind of woman am I?

Cal would divorce her – she would lose the love of her life and it was well deserved.

I can't do that to him.

I can't do that to me.

There was only one choice. Aldi made the appointment at a clinic in Manhattan where no one would recognize her. The physical abortion was fast and easy. Afterward, she stayed in bed for a few days, telling Cal she had the flu. It was sickeningly easy to lie.

Something shifted in Cal. Aldi didn't dare ask what changed. Perhaps seeing her sick terrified him?

"I'll take care of you," he said. "I can't stand the idea of losing you."

He made chicken soup and soft-boiled eggs; brought buttered toast and ice cream with chocolate sprinkles. He held her tightly, saying the words she'd missed for eight long months.

"Aldi, I love you. Aldi, you're beautiful."

Cal was back.

Aldi tried to block out the doctor and the abortion; the smiling nurse that assured her. "Don't worry dear, when you're ready, you'll have a house full of babies."

The words made her shiver. Why was she so weak? Why did she allow The Senator to possess her? For a brief moment, the colors returned; the fire of his body, his tongue, his fingers burning her skin. Her heart pounded and she was again lost in his icy power.

I can never have him . . . and never get rid of him.

Over the years the images retreated until she and Cal decided to have a baby, and they were diagnosed with infertility.

Aldi knew, without question.

It's my fault we can't have children.

Something died inside after The Senator left and she aborted his baby. She had become a brown, lifeless flower surrounded by vivid blooms. God, karma, or some cosmic power was punishing her.

11

Aldi shook the memories from her consciousness. It was eight years ago. Cal wasn't depressed. They had a beautiful Gothic house and a store. *Teach Washington How!* faded permanently from her life.

It was time to call DSS. Move on and stop punishing herself. The DBM letter was dead. Maybe a child would make her forget *forever*?

Aldi made the call. "I'm looking for Kiran," Aldi said to the person who answered the phone.

After a few clicks, a young voice answered. "How can I help you?"

Aldi took a deep breath. "Jaime from William Chain's office suggested that I call. I believe her boyfriend works with yours . . ."

"Yes. They're firemen."

"That's quite a job," Aldi mumbled, not knowing what to say.

"It sure is. I worry more than most, but Morgan is the best guy in the world."

Aldi nodded as if Kiran could see her.

"How can I help you?"

"Aldi," she filled in quickly. "My name is Aldi. Jaime told me you might have some babies or toddlers that need homes."

"Are you a foster parent?"

"No. My husband and I – we want to adopt a child. We thought that this might be another way."

"Of course," Kiran said. "It's very different than going through an agency or attorney."

"I understand. We're qualified – all the paperwork, home studies, courses . . ."

"Can you send me the paperwork? Once I take a look, if everything works, I'll call you and your husband for an appointment."

Aldi found it hard to breathe. "Yes. Do you . . . do you have any babies?"

"Maybe," Kiran said slowly. "I know of a toddler, a little boy, 15 months old, who needs a home."

Aldi couldn't believe the words. "He's available?"

"Yes," Kiran said, "but there are a lot of steps between a phone call and an adoption."

"I understand," Aldi whispered. "I do understand."

"Good," Kiran said firmly. "Now send me the paperwork and I'll see what we can do."

"Thank you." Aldi hung up the phone.

Was it finally happening?

12

Aldi sent the paperwork to Kiran.

Kiran stared at the copies on her desk. She received a strange call from Father.

"You know," Father said, "I'm a personal friend of William Chain."

"Of course. He's been at all our events . . ."

The Senator interrupted her. "I want you to do something for me. A woman will call you about foster parenting. Her name is Aldi."

"You know I can't talk about my clients . . . it's confidential."

Father sniffed. "You'll like this one. She'll fit all your requirements."

"I don't . . ."

"I'm not asking you to *do* anything. Just pay attention. If they suit your . . . standards . . . make sure this couple gets Baby Joshua Doe."

"How do you know about Baby Joshua Doe?"

"I know what I need to know. Do you understand?"

"No."

"It doesn't matter, Kiran. Just do it. Have a nice day."

The Senator cut the connect.

Kiran didn't know what to make of the call, particularly since Aldi and Cal were the perfect couple. No children. Older. Desperate for a baby. They were financially comfortable, well-educated, owned a home, and could understand the troubles of a broken child. It would be a perfect fit.

Why did Father care?

Father must have had an altruistic motive – maybe something to do with the attorney, William Chain? Kiran took a deep breath. It was risky asking Father too many questions. She quickly relegated the conversation to the place, deep inside, that she reserved for Father and her doubts. It was much safer that way. She reached for the phone and called Sharon Candido, who had been waiting for a new placement for Baby Joshua.

"He's getting worse," Sharon said shakily. "More aggressive. The girls are scared. You have to take him out of here."

"How can you be scared of a 15-month old?" Kiran asked.

"Do you really want to know?"

Kiran had nothing to say.

Poor Joshua. Who are you?

"I might have someone," Kiran said slowly. "I just need a little more time."

There was silence on the phone.

"We never touch him," Sharon said slowly. "If we leave him alone he doesn't cry or scream or throw temper tantrums. It's the only way."

Kiran sighed. "I know you're doing your best."

"Maybe," Sharon said softly. "Maybe he doesn't belong in a home with other people . . ." Kiran cut her off. "He's just a baby. It's way too soon to make that call."

Sharon was quiet. "He's broken," she said so softly Kiran could barely hear. "I know it."

She ignored the foster mother's comment. Kiran's next move was to contact Aldi.

"I'd like to make an appointment and meet your husband." Kiran said to Aldi when she picked up the phone.

Kiran heard the tears.

13

Cal squinted at the entrance to the DSS building. He paused. Everything looked dingy and grey.

What am I doing here?

He and Aldi had been through so much and now . . . this?

Adoption? Cal never saw himself as the type to adopt. Yes, he wanted to be a parent; he wanted to make Aldi happy; but a kid with no history? His genetic makeup could be anything. Cal wasn't a scientist, but he was in awe of the human effort that went into genetic research. One shouldn't toy with the human genome. Adopting a child was like stepping into a black hole – totally unknown territory. Books were reliable, value based on content, author, condition, age, and demand in the marketplace. You knew what you were getting. But a child?

Think.

Books could bring big surprises. He had seen that many times since he opened the *Tree of Life*, his antiquarian and rare books business. A $10,000 book may be discovered at a tag sale or thrift shop. A first edition of Charles Darwin's 1859's *The Origin of Species* showed up in a family's guest bathroom in the UK and later sold for $174,000. People often stockpiled first editions that never went anywhere except onto bargain book tables.

Internet speculators made prices go wild, if only for the moment. Everything was predictable until you tripped over that goldmine left in an attic or the bowels of a dusty old basement where someone had forgotten it 50 years ago.

Why should human adoption be any different?

If he and Aldi had conceived he wouldn't have to ask the questions. They tried so hard to have a baby. Cal wanted to continue his family line – he was the only one left who could do it. He shuddered. Eight years, and he still missed his family.

He and Aldi did everything possible to procreate. They had gone from good sex to sex for the sole purpose of making babies, and failed.

Their diagnosis was age-related infertility. It was as meaningless as saying that a worn First Edition had no value. The doctors couldn't find anything specific that made them unable to conceive. It just wasn't happening. They failed a basic biological imperative. He never thought that 38 would be too old to have a baby, but . . .

Cal sighed. He needed to reframe this. Adoption could be a gift to parent and child. It was about people brought together by powerful, unseen forces in the cosmos – an inevitable connect that some called karma, others fate or destiny, and still others a reunification of souls torn apart in a previous life. Cal reviewed the facts dispassionately.

What would the Israelites have been without the adopted Moses? James Michener was a foundling, and Edgar Allen Poe was a foster child. John Lennon was raised by his aunt and uncle, and Edward Albee was adopted when he was two years old. And Nelson Mandela? Perhaps he would be raising the next Nelson Mandela?

Cal grinned and thought of Robert Frost's words, from *The Road Not Taken.*

I took the one less traveled by,
And that has made all the difference.

Maybe this was *his* chance to take the road less traveled? Cal was afraid of the adoption *and* the unknown. Yet every child was an unknown; a parent could love his or her biological offspring only to find that they had turned against them. Think Adolf Hitler, Joseph Stalin, and Osama bin Laden. There were no guarantees.

Yes, Cal thought. My adopted son has to be the best, the smartest, and *mine.*

Cal would do anything to make Aldi happy. He loved and was fiercely dependent on her. Deep inside he knew that he was the one that failed at procreation. While the tests were vague and inconclusive, never pointing fingers, Cal knew the truth.

I failed her. Now that can change.

He filled his mind with books as Aldi led him into the DSS building. He felt the old, smooth leather of a book cover on his fingertips; a title lovingly embossed in gold with pages edged in gilt. He thought of content in words no longer used today, like *insurmountable, censure,* and *culling,* in sentences long and awkward to the modern reader's eyes.

Cal visualized the digital pen of today's editor, slashing words to make a story move faster, language racing in a post-Hemingway attempt at simplicity, leaving florid metaphors to another age. They called those books "page-turners." Cal sighed. Antiquarian books had time and leisure to fill the void of a blank page; the luxury of verbosity; and the precious art of painting ideas and stories with words. Today's mass produced books, written on keyboards instead of paper, wallowed in thin, passing notoriety like the rest of the culture. He longed for the pages of the past; rag content so high they felt more like fabric than paper; bindings constructed by craftsmen not machines. These days, so much was mired in postmodern shallowness that stories, like paperbacks, had been stripped into superficial facsimiles of the past; fragile brown eggshells with nothing inside.

I'll teach my son all of it.

"C'mon," Aldi pulled at his hand. "Stop thinking."

That was like requesting water be dry. Cal never stopped thinking; his mind raced in as many directions as his books, constantly seeking to explain details that eluded him. It was his joy, his passion, and his albatross.

I'll teach my son that, too.

Aldi grabbed his arm. "This is our chance. Maybe our only chance to have a baby and build a family."

He stared at her blankly.

"Wake up," Aldi added impatiently.

Cal had always been in love with books. It was both passion and obsession, shared with his parents and Edmund, who injected their outlier IQs with literature, history, and philosophy – human thought superimposed on the printed page. His father was a philosophy professor at a local community college. His mother was a poet who published regularly in unknown literary journals that paid in copies. His younger brother, Edmund, was intrigued by maps and old atlases, studying geopolitical differences in yesterday's world. Playing global politics in the present millennium held no interest, and was rarely discussed around the dinner table. They had little money, but surrounded themselves with beautiful old things and shelves of books, crowding their tiny house until it was nearly claustrophobic. Cal loved the suede book covers, gilded pages, and carefully-crafted designs of the old books.

Not many people were comfortable around Cal's odd family, except the college faculty and bibliophiles. It never quite mattered. They had each another.

A family of outliers.

His life changed after he met Aldi, married, and had an idyllic European honeymoon. Cal had felt a joy he never experienced before. It was the romantic love he read about in books. Days spent touring and nights in sweaty, heated sex as if they were immersed in a cheesy Harlequin novel; a story that belonged to someone else. They filled themselves with one another, cementing a connection that he identified with an aching cliché.

Soul mates.

Until the accident, and then Cal felt utterly alone.

He winced, recalling the pain, dizzying descent, and months of anguish after the accident. In one instant, his life changed. Aldi opening the door. The police.

"We're sorry to say . . ."

No. It was impossible then, and now. How could so many lives expire in an instant, like names on a chalkboard, living one minute and erased the next? What was the point? Who and what was the guide?

Cal shivered. Because of their deaths, he prospered. He gave birth to the business, opened the store, and bought their Gothic house.

Aldi nudged him. "Cal," she persisted. "Are you with me?"

Cal knew he wouldn't have survived without Aldi. Although it had been eight years ago, the pain was as fresh as if it happened yesterday. He had clung to Aldi like a lost and terrified child; alone in his history. She cradled him; nurtured him back to life. When everything settled, his family entombed in New Montefiore Jewish Cemetery, he tackled what was left of their lives – the books, the house, and a surprisingly large estate, swelled by life insurance money and a settlement from the DWI's estate. Cal took everything and left his job as a history professor at the University.

Aldi nudged him again.

Cal purchased the space at *Poet's Corner*, a small historic shopping area with upscale shops. He chose it because there was a tiny, separate building in the back, a few steps from the rear exit. No one knew exactly why the building existed – some speculated that it was a one room home for the original owner; others claimed it was a tiny art studio; a few said the building had once hidden runaway slaves on the underground railroad. No one knew – the newspapers, documents, and stories had been lost a long time ago. The old, grey building *called* to him.

Cal named his store *Tree of Life* for the mysterious, spiritual connect in time.

"Cal," Aldi raised her voice. "This may be the most important day of our lives. I need you – *here*." Cal didn't hear.

The tiny building behind the store – not much more than a shed – became Cal's office and sanctuary; he filled it with his favorite books, artifacts, and photos of his family, some more than one hundred years old. He bought a desk, a chair, and savored his private space. It was cluttered and unruly, heavy with the safety of *old*, timeworn ideas, and characters, plots, and ancient vendettas that kept him company when he was happy, troubled, or in need.

Tree of Life and his office felt like Boston's *Old Corner Bookstore* – a beautiful shop built after the Great Fire of 1711, on property that had once belonged to the Puritan dissident Anne Hutchinson. It evolved into a publisher, producing works by Henry Wadsworth Longfellow, Harriet Beecher Stowe, Nathaniel Hawthorne, and Ralph Waldo Emerson. The Old Corner Bookstore was a literary treasure, born from fire. Maybe one day, Tree of Life would also become a publisher?

Aldi pinched him.

As an extension of the *Tree of Life,* Cal and Aldi purchased a Gothic house in brick and white trim, which boasted a turret, eaves, a wrought-iron fence, and old-fashioned leaded windows in all shapes and sizes. Cal set up his woodworking shop in the back, creating an endless line of desktop shelves from exotic woods with names like *acacia, huanghuali, monkey puzzle,* and *pardoo.*

The remaining dollars were invested, creating a solid yearly income that paid for the infertility treatments. The business didn't make much money but Cal felt he honored the memory of his family, keeping them close in the graceful stacks of old, beloved books.

Aldi's income was more than enough to cover daily expenses and needs.

As long as he had his books, Aldi, his Gothic house, and *Tree of Life*, Cal was content.

What more did he need?

14

"Adoption," Aldi spoke sternly, like a teacher reprimanding a kid. "Get out of the middle ages and step into today. We're meeting with a DSS worker to see about foster care and adoption."

Cal looked at her blankly.

Aldi faced him, pausing in front of the entrance to DSS. It was busy with people, cars, and buses on the street. Beneath the large blue sign, reading *Nassau County Health and Human Services,* were two strategically placed garbage pails.

Gently, Aldi touched Cal's cheek, speaking to him slowly as if he were a toddler. "We've been over this a million times. We're *infertile.* Our DBM letter is awful. The only way we can have a family is through foster care and adoption. It's going to be like finding Moses in the bulrushes."

Cal shrugged. It was much easier to speculate on antiquarian books than *today.* Everyone recognized that Mark Twain's personal copy of *Huckleberry Finn*, in rare publisher's sheep, was a treasure valued in six figures. Who didn't know that Audubon's *Birds of*

America sold for $8.8 million, or DaVinci's notebook of drawings and scientific writings, *Codex Leicester*, was worth well over $30 million?

Aldi nudged him back to the present. "I'm losing you."

Cal struggled.

"Stop thinking," she persisted.

Cal stared into her dark eyes. They said something very different than her words. Her eyes were tense; struggling to keep things under control.

Aldi laughed; a strange, choking sound. She knew exactly where *he* was. She gave him a quick hug. "Get out of there," she whispered. "You're a century away."

Cal complied. He was always amazed by Aldi's insight. He forced himself back to the present. This was more about her need, than his.

"You want children," Aldi reminded him, stroking his chubby cheek.

Cal nodded obediently.

Aldi straightened his wire glasses and smoothed his tie. She patted the shoulders of his outdated tweed jacket. "This is the only way."

Cal nodded. Yes, he wanted children. A little girl exactly like Aldi or a little boy exactly like himself. He hungered for the continuity he found in books – passed down, through the generations.

Words and books were beautiful things.

Cal nodded. "I'm ready," he said softly, and was repaid with Aldi's grateful smile.

15

Inside, the DSS office was Kafkaesque. The corridors were achingly clean, noisy, and very crowded; a labyrinth of beige walls, cluttered cubicles, and unforgiving fluorescent lights. People swarmed like sheep milling in an overgrazed pasture. Everyone had to first wait on long, numbing lines for security to check and feed each body through an airport-like scanner. Surveillance cameras were everywhere. Once admitted into the domain, plain signs posted directions under the icy stares of uniformed guards. Some directions led to workers behind thick glass; others to an endless assortment of cubicles; people untouched by other people. Screens announced numbers and times; back room security watched everything like bad TV.

"We're here," Aldi said as they paused in front of a heavy beige door with a stainless steel handle, and a sign, *Services to Children and Families.*

Aldi smoothed her clothes. Cal took a deep breath. She smiled. He frowned.

Was this going to be like one of those books donated to the Salvation Army?

"Let's do it," Aldi said thickly.

"We don't have to," Cal said. "We can turn around and . . ."

It was too late. Aldi opened the door. It felt like someone pressed the mute button. The noise of bodies was left outside; the chaos remained in the corridor. As they entered, the heavy door automatically closed and they were greeted with a chest-high counter and a receptionist with red-striped hair and black-rimmed glasses.

"Yeah," she said, peering at them.

"We're here to see Kiran," Aldi replied.

The receptionist smiled warmly like a changeling. "Aldi and Cal?"

Aldi nodded.

Years later, Aldi would wonder why the receptionist knew exactly who they were.

The receptionist pushed a button and in what seemed like seconds, a lovely young woman with caramel-colored hair, clear blue eyes, and slightly-worn designer clothes appeared. She put out her hand.

"I'm Kiran," she smiled.

Aldi liked her immediately. Kiran looked vaguely familiar, but Aldi couldn't place her. She shook Kiran's hand, noting her skin was soft and the grip snug.

Cal nodded, not offering his hand until Aldi poked him. Kiran shook his hand, a small smile on her lips.

"Come with me," Kiran said. She led them past the counter, through a maze of cubicles, until she reached a corner space with pale beige floor-to-almost-ceiling walls, furnished with a desk, computer, filing cabinet, couch, and two chairs. It was the DSS's concept of luxury.

"Sit," she pointed to the chairs.

Kiran settled in her desk chair and pulled a file from an unsteady stack of folders. "I received all the paperwork from your attorney, William Chain," she began. "Everything is in order. He's a very skilled man. Clearly, you meet DSS standards but I have a few questions to ask."

Aldi nodded.

"Why aren't you waiting longer for a response to your DBM?"

Aldi took a deep breath. "It's been a long time. We tried everything but nothing has worked. We're getting older and we want to start our family."

Cal, uncharacteristically, broke into the conversation. "Our family is like a book without words. We have so much to offer, but we're not sure a young Birth Mother would appreciate us. We're well educated, caring, thinking people . . ."

Kiran nodded.

Cal liked her eyes.

Kiran glanced at the folder. "I see that Aldi's family lives nearby, but you lost your family in a car accident, Cal."

"Yes." He spoke thickly. "They were killed in a car accident – my parents and brother. I inherited some money, and we used it to start a business I knew they would love – antiquarian and rare books. It's a living memory to all the books we read, shared, and never got to discuss."

"I'm sorry."

"It was eight years ago," Aldi jumped in, concerned that the family tragedy would affect their chances. "Since then, Cal has done really well in business. We took some of the money and bought a lovely Gothic house with a turret playroom . . . a lot of room for a family to grow. The rest of the money we put into conservative investments so we would always be financially secure."

"I see that," Kiran absently flipped the pages in the file.

"We have a good life," Cal added. "We want a child to share it with us, nurture him or her, show how beautiful the world can be."

He glanced at Aldi to make sure he was saying the right things. Aldi nodded.

Kiran smiled. She asked several more questions, and then slipped in the most important. "Are you willing to take a toddler?"

Aldi and Cal looked at one another. They had never discussed adopting an older child.

"We were thinking about an infant . . ." Cal began.

"Yes," Aldi interrupted, "but a toddler is fine."

Cal looked at her, surprised. Kiran waited.

They were quiet for too long.

"I have a child in mind," Kiran said finally. She was determined to have this work. The last thing Kiran wanted was to place Joshua in an institution. Sharon Candido was done. The conversation with Father flashed briefly in her head.

Aldi grabbed Cal's hand, her eyes sparkling with hope.

Kiran saw everything. Was she looking at Baby Joshua's *forever parents?*

"There are problems," Kiran added, knowing that Joshua's best chance was with parents who understood him.

"What kind of problems?" Cal asked hesitantly.

Kiran took a deep breath. "He's a beautiful, 15 month old toddler. He's walking now. He lives with a foster care family who doesn't want to adopt him; they have two little girls and feel he's too much for them to handle."

Kiran paused. She felt like a salesman.

"Joshua was a *Safe Haven* baby," she continued after a dramatic interval. "His birthparents dropped him off at a police station on the day he was born. By doing so, the law protects the birthparents from any responsibility for their child – they left no name, medical history, or forwarding information. The newborn was clean and healthy in the hospital – no signs of prenatal exposure to drugs or alcohol, and no indication of physical abuse. He spent a week in the hospital because he began to cry and thrash without stopping. The nurses said he was angry. The doctors searched for medical reasons. Nothing was found. One day he stopped. He was quiet. The neonatologist declared him ready, reporting no physical or mental reason to preclude placement and eventually adoption. They noted that Joshua would thrive in a warm, healthy home."

Kiran paused. "He came with this." She handed them the note.

Cal read it over Aldi's shoulder. Aldi gasped. A few words were scribbled on a sticky note.

> Please keep birth note from Joshua's Momma
> with all records. Do not remove – Kiran

Kiran continued. "Clearly, Joshua's biological mother *cared*. For reasons we'll never know, she couldn't keep him. She left her newborn in a place she believed was safe and best for him. The report says he was brought in by an unidentified male, in a picnic basket, wrapped safely in a red checked tablecloth like the ones you find in a pizzeria.

There was an awkward silence as Aldi and Cal struggled to grasp the Birth Mother's intent. Cal's mind shifted to a collage of characters, abandoned by mothers, in books of mystery, terror, and fear.

Kiran's voice broke through the images. "When Joshua didn't do well in his first placement, I removed him with the foster parent's request. I brought him to his second placement. It didn't work there either. They've been waiting for me to find him a new home."

"What's wrong with him?" Aldi spoke softly. Cal tilted his head slightly, trying to fully absorb Kiran's words.

"Joshua doesn't like to be touched. He's removed from other people. He's very calm, as long as you leave him alone. He doesn't seem to notice when there are other kids around. As an infant, he didn't suck well so he was a difficult baby to feed. When he got older, he wouldn't allow anyone to hug him. He's built a cocoon around himself as if afraid that he's going to be abandoned again. Some people call it attachment disorder – a result of his birth mother abandoning him."

Aldi shivered. "How can a mother abandon a child like that?"

Kiran shrugged. "There are far worse scenarios. Parents that abuse or neglect their children; babies found in dumpsters . . . Joshua's mother couldn't do that."

Who was she?

And who was Joshua?

The questions were silently shared among the three adults – never asked out loud.

"Can he be helped?" Cal wondered.

"I believe he can," Kiran said slowly. "He needs gentle, patient parents to make him feel secure. He needs a house where he'll feel safe – we call it a *forever home*. Once he feels safe, Joshua will be fine. It will take time and understanding. The present foster parents don't get that. They don't believe that babies can have feelings. "

Aldi and Cal looked at one another.

"Can you give Joshua his forever home?" Kiran challenged them.

Aldi didn't hesitate. Cal was unsure, but what did he know about children? He let Aldi take the lead.

"Let's meet him," she said firmly.

Kiran smiled. Joshua was like a lone goose, facing a strange, dark world where there was no place for him.

If anyone could help Joshua, it was Aldi and Cal.

If he could be helped.

Forever Home

1

People smile at me. I hate their smiles. People try to play silly games. I hate that, too. It's only a matter of time until they toss me away, like her. Another place. Another set of faces. More piles of toys with sharp edges that cut my skin, drawing blood.

They hurt.

I don't want to feel. I know, beneath all the smiles, they want to kill me. Everyone wants to kill me. Most of the time I keep them away. I don't smile. I don't look at them. I refuse to play. Sometimes they try to hug me and it hurts. Their fingers feel like fire. I scream, but they don't get it. They hug tighter and I scream louder, and still they don't get it. As soon as they back off, I stop and turn away.

Sometimes, the momma named Sharon tries to talk to me.

Joshua, what's wrong? Why don't you like me?

Why don't I like her? Isn't it clear? Don't I make it clear? I hate her touch, hate her attention. How can I let her in? How can I be sure she won't abandon me, like the others?

Please Joshua, let me hug you. Let me love you.

The words are like the rocks in the backyard garden. She throws them at me. Leave me alone. Can't you just leave me alone?

Am I that terrible a mother?

I want to laugh. Are you that terrible? It's your fault I'm here. It's your fault she left me. Everything is your fault.

She gives in. I hear her call a person named Kiran. Kiran hovers in the shadows, waiting for the next disaster. She doesn't try to love me so I like her.

Kiran, you have to find a place for Joshua. I can't handle him. Please help.

I listen to the words. They have no meaning. They don't touch me inside because I have a red checked tablecloth that protects me from everyone so I don't feel.

Kiran comes to visit and speaks softly. You're going to meet your forever parents. Things will be okay.

Am I supposed to believe her? Things will be okay? I laugh. Doesn't she know that things will never be okay? I live in a cocoon made from a red checked tablecloth. I'm old wood left from the fire – dark, charred, and ugly. Burnt forever. My only friend is fire.

No, Kiran, things will never be okay.

2

Kiran made sure that the first time Aldi and Cal met Joshua they were all in neutral territory. She wanted to enhance bonding between child and prospective parents.

They didn't need to see Joshua at his worst.

Sharon Candido brought him into the DSS conference room before Aldi and Cal arrived. The room was less sterile than the office or building that surrounded it; floor-to-ceiling walls were painted institutional green, decorated with children's drawings, and warm-and-fuzzy unframed posters of animals and flowers. There were adult chairs and a cool, but friendly government-issue couch. Child-sized plastic chairs in primary colors surrounded a small play table. Well-used toys were everywhere – a mixture of broken, worn, and donated, along with a pile of brightly colored blocks.

Sharon and Kiran let Joshua explore, not hindering his behavior or touching him.

The receptionist buzzed to inform Kiran that Aldi and Cal had arrived. Kiran left immediately to greet them. She led them to the conference room. "Remember," Kiran advised, "this is all new for Joshua. He's very young and it might frighten him. For now, stand in the doorway and watch until Joshua acknowledges you."

Aldi and Cal agreed nervously, standing in the doorway as if frozen to the floor. Kiran lingered next to them. Joshua didn't know, or care, who they were. Sharon Candido crouched fearfully in the corner.

Aldi sighed. "He's the most beautiful child I've ever seen," she whispered.

Kiran agreed. "Yes he is."

Joshua's caramel-colored hair framed a compelling baby face; large blue eyes peered out at the world. He was tall for his age, with no baby fat, and toddled around the room aimlessly. His foster mother watched at a distance, close enough to grab him if he got in trouble.

"Why was he abandoned?" Aldi asked rhetorically.

Kiran didn't respond.

The questions came rapid-fire. "Who would abandon such a beautiful child? Why hadn't the foster parents kept him? Was this meant to be?" Another question remained unasked.

Is Joshua penance for betraying Cal, aborting The Senator's baby, and living a lie?

"I can fix a broken child," Aldi said softly.

Joshua toddled over to a pile of cars and trucks. He examined them carefully, touched their edges, felt their smoothness, and experimented with their weight.

He found a green tractor. Without a smile or sound, Joshua smashed it against the wall. It didn't break.

Joshua tried again. The toy remained intact. The toddler pounded it against the wall to no avail. He couldn't break it, so he tossed it aside.

Cal winced. "Is that normal? I researched *Attachment Disorder* and it sounds very serious."

"We can fix anything," Aldi mumbled.

"Maybe not."

Aldi was mesmerized, her eyes glazed.

"What do I know about kids anyway?" Cal shuddered.

"He's beautiful," Kiran said softly, ignoring the toy tractor. "That's what makes it so striking. Joshua is beautiful, but rejects the foster people who care for him." She shook her head.

"Can a baby that young have such strong feelings?" Cal asked, not expecting an answer. He watched Joshua move from the green tractor to the blocks. Joshua piled the blocks carefully, as high as he could balance them. Then with one sweep of his fisted hand, he sent them flying in all directions.

"Shouldn't he be laughing?" Cal asked cautiously.

Kiran nodded. "I warned you."

"He needs our help – our love," Aldi mumbled.

Kiran looked at Aldi. "It won't be easy," she sighed, suddenly questioning her decision to introduce Joshua. What if these people couldn't handle him? What if his *forever home* turned out to be his forever jail – as unbearable as his earlier foster placements? What if Joshua couldn't make it? There were so many stories about kids diagnosed with RAD. Diagnoses made *after* the fact, when damage had already been done. Parents who tried so hard to make things right, unknowingly doing all the wrong things.

She thought about the infamous Romanian children who spent the first year of life, malnourished, unattended, and without stimulation in cramped, bare-walled institutions. The images had been on TV, following the Christmas Day execution of Dictator Nicolae Ceausescu in 1989. There were tens of thousands of these children. In a rush of international adoptions, parents believed that food, love, and shelter would immediately fix them.

They were wrong. The kids had problems with attachment, severe developmental delays, and emotional damage. Many banged their heads, rocked back and forth, and had autistic-like symptoms.

Now, watching Joshua, Kiran wondered if he had similar problems.

I warned them.

Not like the Romanians.

Kiran told them the truth. They knew Joshua came with problems. Yet Joshua was younger and American-born. He only spent his first week in an institution at the neonatal nursery in the hospital. After that he was in foster homes, with concerned caretakers. Neither the Fletchers nor Candidos had figured out how to handle Joshua.

Kiran *knew* that Aldi and Cal could give him a better life, win him over, and make him a happy part of a forever home. They were smart, educated, and caring.

She had to believe that.

3

Cal watched Joshua, not sure what he was seeing. Should he be reading between the lines like in a novel?

The child was beautiful. Aldi was already in love with him, but who was Joshua? They had no idea – they would never have any idea. Was he willing to overturn his entire life for this little stranger? Sure, if Aldi had given birth . . . Cal tried to shake the thought from his head. There was no difference between a biological baby and an adopted one. He recalled what one social worker had told them during a home study.

"Having children is a risky venture," she advised quietly. "Adopting children increases the risk. Either way, you love them."

Uncomfortable images scattered his thoughts. Cal rubbed his head, trying to clear his mind. So many emotions; so many questions; he didn't know where to begin. He thought of an E. E. Cummings poem:

> *what if a dawn of a doom of a dream*
> *bites this universe in two*

"Are you okay?" Kiran asked softly.

"Of course I'm okay," Cal said brusquely.

Aldi glanced at him questioningly.

Inside the conference room, Joshua found a truck and flung it against the wall. A black plastic tire snapped off and rolled across the floor. Joshua watched it, mesmerized.

Cal winced.

"Typical terrible twos," Kiran said weakly.

Joshua never smiled. When the tire slowed, and fell flat, Joshua took an armful of blocks and flung them in a rain of bright colors. The tire was quickly forgotten.

Kiran took a deep breath. "Let's go meet Joshua," she forced a smile.

Cal stared at her. The grin reminded him of someone, but he couldn't quite place it. Maybe a customer from Tree of Life?

Kiran led them into the room.

Joshua heard. He looked up and met Aldi's eyes, then returned to throwing toys.

Cal heard Aldi whisper under her breath.

My baby. Finally.

Kiran cautiously introduced them to the foster mother, Sharon Candido, who had a desperate look in her eyes. She smiled and shook hands, glancing at Joshua. Joshua was oblivious to the adults; he was focused on smashing toys.

Kiran was nervous. "How about some introductions?"

Aldi and Cal nodded; Kiran led them to the child.

Joshua looked up and went back to the toys. Sharon Candido smiled anxiously.

Kiran sat on the floor. "Joshua," she said softly, "I want you to meet someone."

Joshua ignored her. Sharon Candido shook her head.

"Joshua," Kiran said sharply, "do you hear me?"

"Maybe he's deaf," Cal said.

Aldi gave him a searing look. Cal was quiet after that.

"Joshua," Sharon knelt next to Kiran. "Please come closer."

"No," Joshua cried in a toddler sneer. "NoNoNoNo."

"I don't know what's gotten into him," Sharon said apologetically.

No one believed her.

Aldi joined the women. "Joshua," she said softly. "I would like to meet you."

The third, strange voice caught his attention. Joshua turned and looked at her, a yellow car in one hand, a block in the other.

"Joshua," Aldi said again.

Joshua was unsure. He glanced at the pile of toys against the wall. Aldi held out her hand.

"Joshua," Aldi said gently.

Joshua acquiesced. He toddled to Aldi, tossing a block at her. She ducked and laughed. Joshua didn't smile; he watched. Aldi opened her arms. Joshua backed away.

"Don't touch him," Sharon warned.

Aldi didn't listen. She took his arm and tried to hug him.

Joshua started kicking and screaming, fighting to get away. "Let him go," Sharon said over the screams, "he'll stop."

Aldi released Joshua. He stopped crying, and ran back to the wall, as far away as possible.

"He doesn't like to be touched," Sharon explained.

There was nothing more to be said.

4

Aldi and Cal sat in a café. It was an American-style bistro, with white linen tablecloths, large windows, and hanging plants in brown wicker baskets. A distressed brick wall, with signed photos of celebrities, completed the ambiance.

Aldi sighed. "You know the note left by Joshua's Momma? The red-checked cloth could have come from the Pizza Baas."

"We could have eaten there," Cal responded.

They were less than a mile from the infamous, refurbished *Pizza Baas* in Freeport. Two years ago, the owner had been found murdered in the storeroom. His wife took over and billed it as a mecca for tourists and ghost hunters – a *haunted* pizzeria.

"The pizza is supposed to be awful," Aldi commented.

Cal smiled. "I wonder what haunted pizza tastes like."

"Someone wrote a book about it. Can you imagine?" Aldi shrugged. The small talk ran out.

Cal stared at the menu, not seeing anything. He selected a Santa Fé chicken wrap with jalapenos and spicy cheese, paired with a bottle of *Pellegrino*. He scanned the bistro, watching other diners like images on a television screen. The young couple dressed in sixties retro jeans and tie dye shirts, held hands. A professional woman alternated taps on her laptop and bites of her Panini. Two businesswomen sat with heads pressed close and brows knitted, as if trading corporate secrets.

He glanced at the brick wall. There was the Great Gatsby smiling from a small movie poster. Bill Clinton was at a desk, signing a copy of his 957-page memoir, *My Life*. Meryl Streep was squeezed into a photo of the owner and staff members, her signature scrawled at the bottom. An assortment of B-actors and celebrities, with signatures across their images, completed the décor.

Aldi reviewed the menu as if she were reading a research paper. "I don't know what to get. What do I want, Cal?"

Cal knew exactly what she wanted, but it wasn't on the menu.

Sighing, Aldi selected a caramelized pecan salad with gorgonzola cheese and mangos sprinkled over mixed heirloom greens.

The waitress took their orders.

Silence hung between them.

Aldi closed her eyes. Cal thought about the store. He'd left his part-time helper, Etan, in charge – a kid from the university who was majoring in ancient Greek history. He liked Etan – he reminded Cal of his brother. Cal knew he could trust the kid, yet he still hated being away during business hours.

"We have to talk," Aldi began.

Cal thought about what had happened in the DSS room.

"He doesn't like to be touched," Aldi said to Cal, reading his thoughts.

The waitress delivered their food.

Cal shook his head and munched on a few chips. "What kind of baby doesn't like to be touched?"

"A hurt baby," Aldi said softly. "A suffering child." She paused. "He's ours now."

"He's not ours *yet*. He won't be easy – Kiran said that."

"Kiran said that she believes we can help him."

"*Think*, Aldi. What do we know about kids? What makes you believe that we can help him and unravel the damage?"

"What damage? He's too young to have any real permanent damage. We can fix him, make him happy, give him parents he can trust."

Cal looked away. "The books say something else."

"Enough with the books!"

Cal looked at her. Aldi never yelled. He didn't respond. He took a large bite from his Santa Fé wrap.

Aldi picked at her salad. "I'm sorry," she said finally. "I didn't mean to yell."

Cal nodded.

"I feel so strongly about this."

"Think about it. We're signing on for life."

"I know this child is for us. I know it was meant to be."

Cal wondered how she could be so sure. What did she see in Joshua that eluded him?

"I feel it," she added, as if reading his thoughts. "I feel it inside, as if something metaphysical has shifted. Do you know what I mean?"

Cal knew what she meant. He simply wondered whether it was a metaphysical shift or the chance to finally have a child. Aldi was desperate for children; she hated watching Beth and her parents revel in the girls, feeling ignored, left out from their inner circle. Was Aldi so desperate that she would accept anyone?

Anything?

"The DBM letter," he said hesitantly, reaching for her hand.

"The DBM letter? Who would want us? Let's be real about it. We're not the typical, happy American couple that you see on TV."

"No, we're not. But we have a lot to offer. Our books, our minds, our intellects . . ."

"Don't you get it," Aldi snapped. "No one cares about *that*. They want pretty and thin, athletic and popular. Not us."

"Beth?" Cal asked softly. Aldi looked away.

There was a long silence.

"The DBM letter is just another ruse – a way for William Chain to collect money," Aldi said finally. "It's not going anywhere."

Cal stared at his plate, playing with an errant jalapeno. "Chain said we had a chance."

"Chain is full of himself. Kiran is a better adviser." Aldi paused. Her voice changed. "Do you think you can *love* Joshua?"

Cal didn't answer. He needed time. The child was beautiful but something was missing. He couldn't quite define it. Perhaps Kiran's explanation was correct – Reactive Attachment Disorder. He would have to do more research. With all of that, could he love the tiny, fragile little boy so hurt by life?

"Of course," Cal conceded. "Of course I can love Joshua."

"That's all that counts," Aldi said firmly. She squeezed his hand and released it, taking a forkful of salad. "We'll make him better."

Cal watched her eat. He loved her so much. He would do anything to make his beloved wife happy.

Anything.

5

They went home.

Cal slipped into his workshop. It was his safe room.

The walls were finished in beige and filled with meticulously organized cabinets, pegs, and tool storage areas. The largest piece was an oak woodworker's bench, with a vise at one end. There was a smaller workbench and a large, rolling metal cabinet that held nails, screws, blades, utility knives, and bits. His power tools were stored safely in a large standing cabinet – power drill, random orbital sander, circular saw, and compound miter saw. Most of his hand tools hung from hooks on a peg board, including screwdrivers, hammers, tape measure, and level.

His favorite tool was a claw hammer that had belonged to his father. The hammer had a smooth, slightly rounded head with a sharp curling claw. The handle was a special red polymer material for a good grip. Sometimes Cal stared at the hammer, thinking about his father and the years he spent tinkering in his much smaller workshop. Cal's father had never produced anything of great value. Cal remembered him standing at his cluttered workbench, claw hammer in hand, swinging gently at nails. The sound of the hammer, the smell of the wood, his father humming a soft melody while he worked, were all permanently imprinted in Cal's memory.

Cal was in the process of making yet another Roycroft-style free standing bookshelf. When finished, it would hold about eight volumes. Sometimes, he would make shelves and sell them at the store; other times he gave them away as presents. His favorites peppered his workshop, creations that he refused to part with. There was the shelf made from acacia wood, another made from grey recycled Barn wood, and just beyond was the delicate Olive wood, so costly to purchase.

Cal picked up the claw hammer, ready to work. Instead, he stood there staring at the red handle his father once held. Holding the hammer was like shaking his father's hand – it was a tool that drifted from the past.

Did he dare pursue the adoption?

Did he dare not *pursue the adoption?*

Reactive Attachment Disorder sounded more like a sentence than a diagnosis. What did it really mean? He thought of Aldi's words.

What damage? He's too young to have any real damage. We can fix him, make him happy, and give him parents he can trust.

Can you fix a child like you fix a bookshelf? Cal stared at the claw hammer in his hand.

Can you answer that, Dad?

There were no answers, only questions that plagued him; questions that Aldi refused to acknowledge. She wanted a child so badly she was willing to risk anything. Cal raised the claw hammer and hit a nail in his latest project.

The nail bent beneath the hammer.

6

Aldi went to the kitchen. Although they had already eaten, she took out her butcher block cutting board. She grabbed red and yellow peppers from the refrigerator, along with an onion. She stared at the vegetables.

Chopping relaxes me.

Chop. Chop. Chop.

Aldi slipped her favorite eight-inch chef's knife from the block. It was a *Henckels* – a German company founded in 1731 and known as one of the world's leaders in knives. Her prized knife was a *Forged Premio*, an elegant, three-rivet design with a black handle, satin finish, and expertly forged steel blade. She raised the *Forged Premio* like a weapon; the vegetables were her prey. Aldi's knife flew rapidly through the air, moving as if to a metronome. The silver blade flashed in the dying rays of the sun. Up down. Up down. Bits of red pepper, yellow pepper, and purple onion became tiny, mangled pieces. She diced more vegetables, not quite seeing how much she was doing.

What should I do about Joshua? Was it meant to be?

Her own words danced to the beat of the knife.

He's too young to have any real damage.

We can fix him, make him happy, and give him parents he can trust.

Are children fixable? Was little Joshua a bad seed? She thought about his silky, caramel-colored hair and compelling blue eyes.

A child that beautiful can't be bad.

Aldi set down her chef's knife, laying it across the butcher block. She stared at the knife, as if it could give her the answer. The house was oddly silent. A chill ran through her as she recalled the Birth Mother's note.

Aldi took a deep breath. "I'll give your son a safe haven, Joshua's Momma," she said out loud to no one. She stroked the knife. "I'll love him and make sure he has a better life than you."

7

Aldi and Cal met with Joshua three more times – twice at DSS and once at Sharon Candido's home. Then they were invited to do an overnight.

Everyone was nervous.

Aldi spent a few weeks searching for a crib that would eventually turn into a youth bed. She prepared Joshua's room – a large, sunny space with pale sage green walls and oak wood floors, next to the turret playroom. The walls were bare. Aldi didn't want to do anything more until Joshua was actually theirs. Green shutters covered the windows and a new wood crib was set against the wall.

Cal made his own preparations. He put a lock on the door to his dark, mahogany panelled study. The room held some of his favorite volumes, many worth hundreds of dollars. The desk and shelves were cluttered with antiquarian objects – Roycrofter furniture and carved leather, tiny Israeli artifacts, framed renaissance book illuminations, and small trays made from African woods. He would make sure to transfer anything that was really important or valuable to his office at *Tree of Life*. He didn't want to take chances with his most treasured things.

"How do you baby-proof a Gothic house?" Aldi sighed.

Cal shrugged. He had no clue.

Kiran made a long visit, and laughingly told them what they needed to remove, raise high, or block off with child gates. Aldi was amazed by the amount of work.

"Children aren't easy," Kiran said.

"Joshua will be," Aldi grinned.

"I doubt it," Kiran frowned. "You're going to have to work very hard."

Cal wondered if Aldi had noticed that in their visits, Joshua always kept his distance. At first, he watched them warily as he went about his play, smashing toys, throwing things, or toppling blocks. Cal saw the anger and was amazed that a child so young could be so intense.

I can learn to love him, Cal concluded. Like all those great men in history who emerged from their private fires.

Aldi just smiled.

The first overnight was chilling. Joshua went into his "room" and explored, as they watched him from the doorway. He looked confused, babbling odd sounds that had no meaning. When Aldi tried to break into his world, Joshua responded with anger – screaming, crying, and flailing the air with his arms. She backed off.

"He'll get used to us," Aldi said with confidence.

Cal had his doubts.

Joshua settled into a corner and began to rock, singing baby-talk songs that comforted him.

"Does that mean he's autistic?" Cal asked.

Aldi turned her anger on him. "He's been tested," she retorted. "He's not autistic – just scared, alone, and angry."

Cal had no experience with children, so he backed off. Without realizing what he was doing, Cal also backed off from Joshua, establishing a safe distance between them.

Joshua didn't care.

Aldi didn't notice.

"He'll be ours soon" Aldi said softly.

Cal shook his head.

The balance shifted during Joshua's last overnight, as if the toddler had accepted his fate.

Cal built a small fire in the fireplace in the den. He protected it with a new burnished black iron baby-proof screen. He was careful to move the long fireplace matches, tool set, and fatwood out of the toddler's reach. He dimmed the lights and sat on the floor with Aldi. The room was cozy, flickering in the light from the flames. Joshua wandered among shiny new toys until his eye caught the fire. He toddled over to the screen and sat, mesmerized by the flames. Aldi and Cal leaned against the overstuffed, flower print couch, watching and waiting. As the fire began to die, Joshua turned to them. He stared. Then he picked up a children's book and went to the couch.

"Read," Joshua demanded.

They couldn't touch him; they couldn't cuddle him. Joshua sat on the floor as they read him a story about an adopted dog named Gizmo. It was called *Gizmo Gets His Wish*.

Aldi finished the story, her face soft in the flickering light.

Our families come from many places.
Even our pets come from around the world.

We live, work, and have fun together.
That is what makes our world so special.

Cal watched Joshua. He waited for the toddler to smile or clap his hands. He waited for any reaction. Instead, Joshua turned and stared at the dying embers in the fireplace.

8

The woman Kiran says this is my forever home. Forever? Nothing is forever.

The brick walls outside terrify me. Inside, the woman named Mommy and the man named Daddy show me my room. It's pale green. There is a cage with wood bars. They try to touch me.

No!

Don't touch me!

How can these new people hurt me? Kill me? Her memory fades into a dark hole, where it takes root. The others can't touch me. She has made sure of that.

I keep the first people out. I keep the second people out. Now, I have forever people. I will find a way to keep them out too.

The walls of my cocoon get thicker every day.

Joshua, Kiran says, meet your Mommy and Daddy. They love you.

Joshua, the woman called Mommy says I love you.

The man called Daddy says nothing.

I don't want anyone to love me. I want to crawl inside myself, sing my songs, and not hear the words or sounds of other people. I don't want to hear them breathing; I don't want to feel their touch; I don't want to wither under their scalding eyes, trying to trap me.

I want to be alone.

I deserve to be alone. I was sent away because I'm bad; horribly, hopelessly bad. I don't deserve love. I know that from the black hole inside. She tells me that every day. I don't want love. Love is ugly and hurts.

Joshua is evil.

Joshua is the demon child.

No one can love Joshua.

I chop the words inside; smash them like the toys I throw against the wall. I need to break everything so no one can touch.

No one.

I hate them and they hate me.

Don't touch me!

I see a tiny bit of hurt in the woman's eyes. Hurt? I can hurt someone? I think about that. People like her have always hurt me. Do I have the power to hurt someone?

If I can't love, can I hurt?

That makes me feel very good. I throw a truck. It smashes into tiny pieces.

It makes me feel good.

Broken makes me feel good.

The woman named Mommy comes close, and I turn away. She sighs. Sad. Unhappy.

That makes me feel good, too.

She pauses, not knowing what to do.

Let him be, the man named Daddy says to her.

Will you hug me, the woman named Mommy asks?

No!

I hug myself. I crawl into a corner and hug myself. If I hum and sing my songs, I can't hear them. If I close my eyes I won't see them. If I don't let them touch me I won't feel them.

I'm sorry, the woman named Mommy says.

Sorry? For what?

I'll make you happy, Joshua. I promise.

She is begging me? I look at the man named Daddy. He's shaking his head. Is he making the same promise? I laugh inside. Laugh at both of them. Don't they know? Don't they get it?

We'll do fun things together, the woman named Mommy continues. I'll show you love, Joshua. I already love you. And you will love me.

The words attack me. Don't say them! I don't want to hear them. I don't want to believe them. They can never be truth. I can't feel. I won't feel.

I love you Joshua.

I break into the only protection I have against her words. I scream; I cry; I throw things in every direction. The woman named Mommy backs away. I scream louder, fire bursts in my body. The woman backs away even further. It feels good. It feels right.

I control them.

Kiran is here. She talks too much, but doesn't try to touch me. I accept Kiran as part of the landscape.

Ignore the temper tantrums, Kiran says. She calls them terrible twos.

The man named Daddy says yes.

Yes! Leave me alone. Don't tell me you love me. I scream louder, throwing everything within my reach.

The woman named Mommy nods. For a moment I see something delicious in her eyes.

Fear?

We're going to make this work, she says, trying to comfort me.

I scream more. Don't you understand? It can never work for me? She *made sure of that. But they don't understand. They don't want to understand.*

I don't know why I'm in this house, bedroom, or behind wood bars. I don't know why I'm here. I don't even understand when Kiran says this is a forever home. What is forever? I don't get it. I don't want to get it. I want to be alone, so no one can touch me. I want to hear my own voice, feel my own breathing, stroke my own skin – not share with others who will hurt. Don't come into my world, and I won't come into yours.

Later, when I almost sleep, the woman named Mommy and the man named Daddy pick me up and put me in the wood cage.

Sweet dreams *she says.*

Good night *he says.*

I'm too tired to fight.

Tomorrow I'll begin again.

9

Cal sat in his private office in the building behind the Tree of Life. It was very still and he wanted to think away from Aldi and Joshua. The store was closed and he lingered, alone. He reviewed his life, leaching comfort from the nights spent with Aldi in Europe. It was all in the past, like his books and mementos, filling up space in his office and his heart.

Why now?

Joshua was about to permanently enter their lives and Cal was afraid. The present was a slippery thing, creeping up from the past. To understand *why,* look back not forward. It was the only way. For Joshua, the past was dark, a book without words. The child only had a mother who abandoned him and a legacy of a wrinkled napkin on a red-checked tablecloth. Cal shuddered. He had lost his family but they remained in his memory, helping him choose his path. Joshua had no memories.

Cal's fingers rested on an old red book on his desk. He had pulled it from the store shelves, and before he went home, Cal would return it. He didn't want anyone to know what he had read. The hardcover was worn, the red dulled in several places. It wasn't a beautiful volume; no gilt, leather covers, or graceful engravings. It was just a book – a First Edition from 1921, published by A&E Black, London.

The Book of Saints: A Dictionary of Servants of God Canonised
by the Catholic Church: Extracted from the Roman
& Other Martyrologies

Cal wasn't exactly sure why he pulled the book from the shelf. It was an impulsive act. He didn't know whether to believe in God, karma, gilgul, or cosmic forces. They were questions that eluded him; he stayed away from issues that brought him back to his parents and Edmund. Yet he was compelled to check out this book, compiled by The Benedictine Monks of St. Augustine's Abbey, Ramsgate England. He had remembered a name:

Saint William of Rochester, Patron Saint for Adopted Children.

The 12th century saint came with all the trappings of canonization – miracles, pilgrimages to his tomb, holy cures, and donations in his memory. Pope Innocent IV had canonized him in 1256 – a cause pursued by Lawrence de San Martino, Bishop of Rochester. That wasn't the story that called to Cal.

William was a wild young man until he reached adulthood and devoted himself to God. He was a baker, and felt great empathy for poor and neglected children, donating every tenth loaf he baked. One day, on his way to mass, William found an abandoned baby. He named the baby David and adopted him.

Years later, William and David went on a pilgrimage to the Holy Land. They stopped to rest in Rochester, England. Suddenly, David turned on his adopted father – clubbed him, cut his throat, robbed the dead body, and fled. Because William was murdered on a holy journey, he was considered a martyr. After his murder, there were many miracles credited to William's remains.

Cal turned the story over and over in his head. An image popped into his mind – the cemetery at St. James Place in

Manhattan. It was the first cemetery of the Spanish and Portuguese Jews who had come to New Amsterdam in 1654, forming a congregation called Shearith Israel. Originally much larger, only a small remnant remained. Most of the bodies had been removed by the city in 1855. Towering buildings surrounded the old burial ground, their walls scarred and dirty; dull windows overlooked the tiny time-stamp. There were a few trees, flowers, and bushes that struggled to guard the space. Cal had been startled by a crumbling tombstone, words worn away, with three birds balanced on the edge.

Me? Aldi? Joshua?

Fragile birds waiting for . . . who? Cal knew that Aldi had ancestors buried there.

What did the birds and old tombstone have to do with the saint murdered by his adopted son? Was it an omen – a message from Aldi's relatives warning Cal against adopting Joshua? Cal shook his head.

Were Joshua and David the same?

Beyond Birth

1

The Senator paused regally at the entrance to Tree of Life. Cal saw him and immediately rushed over to greet his most favored customer.

"Good to see you, Senator." Cal smiled obsequiously.

The Senator cleared his throat as if making an announcement before a joint session of Congress. "Today, I have something for *you*."

Cal grinned like a little boy. He was totally charmed by the man, like everyone in the country.

"I'm not buying books," The Senator continued. "I understand you have a new son so I came to congratulate you."

"Thank you," Cal momentarily lowered his eyes, humbled by The Senator's attention.

The Senator flashed his media smile. "You don't have to thank me. This is a gift for father and son. I have two children – twins – and they're also part of the story."

"Yes, I know. You're a role model for all fathers."

The Senator nodded. "I try to be – that's why you deserve this gift. You waited a long time to grow your family. Adoption is blessed by God. We're all grateful to people like you."

People like me? Cal wondered how The Senator *knew*. "Aldi and I are very happy."

"Joshua won't be easy," The Senator said ominously.

Cal flinched. Was The Senator trying to tell him something?

"I *know*," The Senator added, God-like. "Believe me."

Cal was afraid to ask anything.

"You're a Jew. It's your lot."

"*What?*"

The Senator ignored Cal's response. He gave the bookseller a beautiful package wrapped in baby boy paper and a blue bow.

Cal tried to ignore The Senator's words. The Senator was everyone's hero, and Cal didn't want to think otherwise.

The Senator's pale, caramel-colored card was taped to the gift. The card had black embossed letters and a line drawing of an American flag.

Direct from the USA White House.
A gift to my very special friend

The Senator's unmistakable signature was printed at the bottom. Cal didn't know what to say.

"Best wishes to you and your wife," The Senator spoke evenly, adding his classic parting statement. "Thank you. Thank you. Thank you."

Cal watched as The Senator turned and slunk back into his chauffeur-driven black *Lincoln* at the curb. Cal was awestruck. The Senator had noticed him and his small family; and took the time to give them a gift. Perhaps Cal had been wrong about Joshua – maybe this was an omen that the adoption was meant to be, and as Kiran said, would turn out fine. Cal took a deep breath and smiled, clutching the package to his chest. The Senator's words echoed in his head.

Joshua won't be easy.

You're a Jew. It's your lot.

Cal thought of David and St. William of Rochester. He saw Joshua smashing toys against the wall and Sharon Candido fearfully crouching in the corner. What was The Senator trying to say?

Cal pushed the images away, replacing them with the child sitting still, mesmerized by the flames in the fireplace.

The Senator, Kiran, Aldi, Joshua . . . Cal sensed a connection, but as in a novel where a reader can only guess at the twisted ending, Cal resigned himself to the unknown. In the years ahead, he would ask the same questions, over and over, struggling to understand which part of the plot he missed.

Cal shook his head and returned to his books. Later that night, after the store closed, he brought the gift home so Aldi could see how The Senator had honored them. Cal and Aldi sat in the den while Joshua stared into the fireplace. Cal presented the gift.

"It's an adoption gift from The Senator," Cal explained. "He told me that 'Adoption is blessed by God. Everyone is grateful for people like us.' Isn't that amazing?"

Aldi frowned. "No, it isn't amazing. You act like that's a big deal. I can't stand the man."

"The Senator? How do you know him?"

"From my *Teach Washington How* days." She said quickly.

"I thought you liked him."

"Until I got to know him."

"He did say," Call added softly, "that Joshua won't be easy – but we're Jews. It's our lot."

Aldi made a strangled sound. She grabbed the gift and pulled off the paper, ripping The Senator's card into pieces. "It's a book. Why would he give *us* a book?"

Cal shrugged, took the book from her hands, and saw the title.

Murder at Pizza Baas

Cal turned the book over and read the back cover blurb out loud.

> Sal, the owner of The Pizza Baas in Freeport, Long Island, was found in a pool of blood, his throat slit, and his body left in the storeroom. The brutal murder remains unsolved. Many believe the shop is haunted. Ghost hunters hang out, hoping to see Sal's apparition, hungering for truth.

The book was illustrated with odd paintings. The most prominent was a dead tree and a painted skull.

"Local legend," Cal said lamely.

Aldi was trembling. "Throw it out," she hissed.

"Why? It's signed by The Senator. The book might be worth something." He turned to the front page where The Senator had written a message:

> *Grow up well, Joshua. Your beauty outside*
> *only matches your beauty inside.*

Aldi's face turned an odd, sickly color. "Get rid of it! I don't care what it might be worth. I *hate* that man."

Cal was surprised by her ferocity. "I'll keep it at the store." He turned to the title page. Instead of the name of the book or author, it had a date.

"No. Throw it out – burn it. I don't want Joshua to ever read it . . ."

"Interesting," Cal said slowly, ignoring her. "The Pizza Baas owner was murdered on the same day Joshua was born."

Aldi screamed. She grabbed the book from Cal. "My God," she whispered. "Oh my God."

She rushed from the room and up the stairs. Cal and Joshua stared at her. "Who can figure out a woman?" Cal said to his son. Joshua didn't respond. He turned and gazed at the flames.

2

The Jews were fucked and The Senator was pleased.

Baby Joshua Doe belonged to Aldi and Cal. The Senator had made it happen, manipulating Kiran and his old friend, William Chain.

The Senator sat in his favorite luxury recliner – a custom-made power seat in dark mahogany leather. It was nestled in his spacious office on Park Avenue. No one entered the office but him, the cleaning lady, and his staff. His wife, daughter, son, and visitors were prohibited without invitation. Requests were filed with his secretary – a stern, homely woman who never smiled. She resided in a large waiting room, filled with his framed campaign posters, community service awards, political commendations, plush seats, and a muscled, uniformed security guard during work hours.

The Senator believed in the domino theory, calculating that one human action will predictably lead to another, given the right context. Remove one piece and everything comes to a dead halt. Keep the flow and events follow like a chain of dominos, each one pushed down and in turn, pushing down its neighbor.

He controlled the game. If there was a problem, The Senator would step in and make it right. He had the power and money to do anything he wanted; target anyone he chose.

The Senator's mark was Espie and her family.

The story began long before he was born, when 15th century Jewish sisters killed his people. The Senator appreciated the ancient vendetta that had been passed down through his bloodline. It was right for himself and his kin. Whether today or 500 years ago, The Senator was destined to play the game. Fortunately, one didn't need to murder with knives and guns anymore. The kill required his intelligence, cunning, and dominoes. The Senator's objective was simple – fuck the Jews and win the game.

Only once did he lose the game; only once when the dominoes flew out of his control. The Senator would never forget or forgive the skirmish.

Known as "DutchBoy," The Senator wore the nickname proudly in his Levittown, Long Island neighborhood where he spent his adolescence. The Jew across the street, Tamirah, had given him the name. She was hot for him and he accommodated her out of pity. They "played" in his bedroom – Tamirah on her knees as he taught her how to service him. Tamirah obeyed without question.

Tamirah's best friend was Hanya, the Jew who lived next door. Hanya's sister, Esperanza – known as "Espie" in the neighborhood – caught his eye. He quickly learned that Espie and his own family tree had been entwined since those 15th century murders. It was pre-ordained that Dutchboy would own Espie.

Red-headed Espie did the unthinkable. She rejected him.

The Senator demanded payback. It didn't matter how much time it would take. He was a patient man. He turned the dominoes in a new direction and waited.

Espie's daughter was Aldi; it was easy to own her.

The brilliant play was to take Joshua, the demon-boy, son of Mack and The Senator's grandson, and make him Espie's grandson.

The Senator laughed out loud.

"Espie," he said to no one, "you should have fucked me when you had the chance. Now your family is doomed."

3

The Senator dozed, a skeletal leer on his face. He dreamed of babies and pizza, pirate ships and Spanish Inquisitors. Flames roared through his mind, lulling him into a dark and comfortable slumber.

Suddenly, he was startled awake. The door flew open and she stood there, rigid with anger, a book clutched in her hand.

It had been a long time, and her anger aroused him.

"Teach Washington How," The Senator said in a singsong voice.

"Why did you do it?" Aldi hissed.

He stared at her coolly. Aldi raised her fist as if she was in a public protest.

The Senator rearranged his face, and donned his political smile. "What are you talking about?"

"You know what I'm talking about. Why did you give him the book?"

"Who?"

Aldi took a deep breath. "Cal. Why did you give Cal *this* book?" She waved *Murder at Pizza Baas* in the air.

"It's a lovely book."

"It's a book about murder."

"Not just any murder."

"I don't get it," she sneered. "Why are you involved?"

"You should get it, my dear. You're a murderer, too."

"What do you mean?" Aldi's voice quivered, her heart pounded, and she was afraid her knees would buckle.

The Senator grinned. "You murdered my baby, remember?"

"How do you know . . .?"

"I know everything."

"I tried to reach you . . . tell you I was pregnant . . ." She stopped, desperate to find the right words.

The Senator shrugged and raised his voice, mimicking the chants of pro-lifers. "Murder . . .murder . . .of the unborn." He frowned like a disgruntled teacher. "Do you know what J.R.R. Tolkien said?"

Aldi shook her head, unable to speak.

"Of course you don't," The Senator chided. "Here goes – 'even the smallest person can change the course of the future.'"

"What are you saying?" She whispered.

"Isn't it obvious, Aldi? You murdered my child and destroyed the future. I've rewarded you with a demon-child . . . Joshua."

"Joshua isn't a demon child."

The Senator snorted.

"I don't understand."

"You will."

Aldi opened the book to the title page.

"Joshua was born the same day that the Pizza Baas owner was murdered."

"So?"

"Are you trying to tell me something?"

"Joshua is in his – what do you call it – *forever home.*"

"Yes."

The Senator laughed – a thin, inhuman cackle.

"You have what you want, Aldi. A baby. Why ask questions?"

The Senator chose a domino from the box and rubbed it slowly between his fingers.

"It really doesn't matter who you fucked to get here."

Years of guilt coursed through Aldi; a tsunami of emotions she hoped had been buried. "You're not going to tell Cal?" She asked hoarsely.

"Maybe I will . . . maybe I won't. I don't know why you even want to keep your puny husband and demon child. It all depends . . ."

"Demon child? Don't call Joshua *that.*"

The Senator licked the domino.

"What do you know that I don't know?" Aldi begged.

The Senator glared at her, his eyes gleaming. "I know a lot. I control everything."

"Please, tell me . . ."

The Senator was silent.

"What . . . do you mean by 'it all depends . . .'?"

The Senator stared at her, God-like. "Now you're getting the picture – realizing who is in control."

Aldi hung her head. "What do you want?"

"Do me," he said lightly.

The color drained from Aldi's face.

"On your knees, kike," his voice hardened, "or the truth will come out. About everything."

Tears coursed down Aldi's face. "You wouldn't . . ."

"No? Imagine the outcome. Your husband will shun you – divorce you for adultery. The country will turn on you – I'll make sure they believe that you drugged me without my knowledge and seduced the beloved Senator, only to cruelly abort his baby." The Senator chuckled. "You'll lose Joshua."

Aldi's head spun with agonizing images. She would do anything to keep Joshua.

Anything.

Aldi closed her eyes, trying to wipe out the scenario. She prayed frantically to God, karma, and unknown cosmic forces to make this all go away.

Nothing happened.

"Now," The Senator roared. "Before I change my mind and you've lost your chance."

Aldi had no choice. She approached him, moving in slow motion, her heart aching and her stomach lurching.

"On your knees," he ordered.

Moaning, Aldi fell to her knees in front of him. He unzipped his pants.

"Do me, kike."

Ayla hung her head. "Why me, Senator?"

The Senator was silent, aroused by her anguish. He didn't respond. Ayla tossed the book aside. One word lingered on her lips.

Why?

Check out the next book in the series

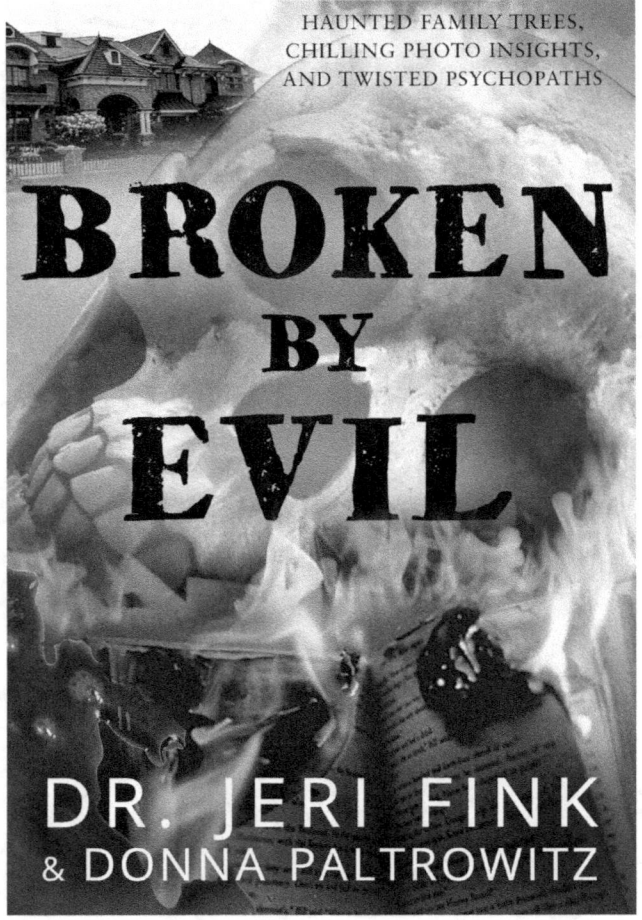

HAUNTED FAMILY TREES,
CHILLING PHOTO INSIGHTS,
AND TWISTED PSYCHOPATHS

BROKEN BY EVIL

DR. JERI FINK
& DONNA PALTROWITZ

Broken By Evil

Joshua is growing up. Strange things happen when the boy is around – dead animals, fires, and terrified kids. How do Aldi and Cal handle their child? How does the school react? Is Kiran still around? Grandma Espie's secrets are revealed as Joshua acts out his psychopathic legacy.

Broken By Evil can be purchased in ebook or print book at
www.amazon.com

Discover more haunted family trees, chilling photo insights,
and twisted psychopaths in:

The first book in the series finds media psychologist, Dr. H (Hanya) and great-niece/ intern, Sage, in Manhattan. Dr. H is a TV psychologist with her own talk show. A psychopath rises from the audience, with a gun and vendetta. Book 1

Go back to 17th century New Amsterdam and meet the ancestors of Joshua, Sage, Hanya, and The Senator. How does a psychopath terrify an entire community? What does Jew's Alley have to do with Hanya's condo? Book 4

Plunge back to the 1490s and its unspeakable horrors. Trace the legacy of Joshua, Hanya, Sage, and The Senator, as they wander through the brutal streets of Lisbon. Book 5

Meet psychopathic soldier, Simao, and follow Esperanza when she's kidnapped and sent to Sao Tome, Africa. Discover the bloody 15th century murder that began it all. Book 6

It's 1492 and the Tapiadors (Secret Jews) are betrayed to The Inquisition. Armed soldiers arrest them. The two daughters escape via a tunnel while the parents are dragged to torture cells. Will they survive the horrors that pervade Spain? Book 7

*Book 2: **Broken By Birth**
Book 3: **Broken by Evil

Books can be purchased in eBooks or print books at:
www.amazon.com

Meet The Book People

Dr. Jeri Fink,
Author and Photographer

I was eight years old.

Faces were penny candy – endless shapes and flavors. Colors throbbed in rhythmic neon lights. My world was a rush of stories written in black-and-white composition books.

There were so many ways to *see* things. The Oak outside my window was big and powerful – or shaky, like a typical New York City tree. I could take a sliver of black charcoal and make the same tree magically come alive on paper. My characters moved through plots more animated than the people next door. I aimed my camera and shot images that no one else noticed.

They called me a free spirit.

I wanted to share, but most of my friends were in different spaces. We went to college and they talked about business, teaching, and making money. I wanted to know about art, lucid dreaming, and the human spirit. We grew up, got jobs, and evolved into families. There were spouses and children; Little League and PTA. I had my family, a home in the suburbs, and a family room painted purple. When everyone dined on backyard barbeque, I preferred Chinese noodles. I stashed chocolate fudge brownie ice cream to weather blizzards, and talked about books no one read at the neighborhood dinner parties.

I never quite *fit*.

I went back to school and became a Family Therapist to help people negotiate their lives. I worked with everyone from "normal" to psychopath. My friends thought *I* was crazy.

Oddly, I was always ahead of my time. I played on the internet before most people had ever heard the word. I developed, along with a group of far-reaching thinkers, the idea of psychotechnology – the psychology of technology. My nonfiction book, *Cyberseduction*, was written long before eHarmony and match. com went viral. Donna Paltrowitz and I worked with kids on books where children became a voice in their own literature. We called the series *The Gizmo Books*. Gizmo and his "sister" Coco were Labradoodles – an Australian breed which most people at the time, including the vet, never knew existed.

Instead of simply growing up, my eight year old *evolved*. In my twenty-eight books I've explored nonfiction, children's, and adult fiction. I'm still fueled by faces, colors, and stories in my world.

The *Broken Book* series is a culmination of who I am – the voices of those who entered my mind and heart; the people who pass me on different paths, with their own haunted family trees; and the photos that tell their stories.

Welcome to my world.

Visit me at www.hauntedfamilytrees.com
Email me at jeri@hauntedfamilytrees.com
Purchase our books at www.amazon.com
Join my photo insights email list at
www.hauntedfamilytrees.com/landing-page

Donna Paltrowitz,
Author

I won!

It was a school writing contest for the best autobiography, and mine came in first. I was in the sixth grade and had no clue about writing. The words flowed effortlessly from my head to the pen. The teacher described my essay as an intricate process rich with ideas, humor, and the desire to connect with others.

Years later, I graduated from college, worked as a teacher in Brooklyn, N.Y. and realized that teaching children to express themselves wasn't the seamless process that I had envisioned. This was a different generation with needs that required new techniques and resources. Spending my days in the classroom with children, and nights earning a Master's Degree in reading, I discovered the latest, most effective techniques to make the entire room smile.

I became a reading specialist. My ideas flowed into developing tools to motivate struggling readers. Focusing on real experiences that kids encountered in their schools, streets, and homes, I created a humorous reading series for children with limited reading vocabularies. Along with my husband Stuart, also a New York City teacher, we wrote the *I Hate To Read Series* – 24 books with music, rhymes, and smiles – long before rap and Miss Piggy became a hit.

We connected with children throughout the country and the English-speaking world. Subsequently, we wrote the *Work World Series* for teenagers trying to make sense of their lives. When schools finally wired up, we designed *Computer Crossroads* and *Mystery Mazes—* software series that engaged young people in reading, laughing, and making fun choices.

Watching my own three children grow up, I realized that reading connections continually evolve. While teachers and administrators tried to lead children to relevant topics, kids were more interested in what their peers were saying. Children connected when they were given a voice. Dr. Jeri Fink, my friend, neighbor, and a LI family therapist agreed that children should have the chance to bring their own literature to life. Together we brought children's issues, words, and artwork alive in *The Gizmo Books*. We visited classrooms with Gizmo, a 100 pound therapy dog and his "sister," Coco. The Labradoodles came from Australia, driving their messages to connect children, parents, grandparents, and schools half way around the world.

Meanings of words shift with the passage of time while the human need to connect remains unchanged. What was once called interacting with friends, neighbors, and colleagues, is now social networking—sharing our messages, bonding with others in the world, and helping us all to feel warm and fuzzy on the inside. Both the teacher and child inside me continue to seek new pathways into the present, as well as the past. That is the heart of *The Broken Book Series*-stories rich with ideas, photos, and the desire to connect with others. Whether child or adult, our families bind us to the good, the bad, and the ugly of our histories. Wander through these adult novels for an insightful connection to the haunted family trees that make us who we are.

Visit us at www.hauntedfamilytrees.com
Email me at donna@hauntedfamilytrees.com
Purchase our books at www.amazon.com

Derek Murphy,
Book and Cover Designer

Derek Murphy started a book editing company while working on his PhD in Literature, but soon began using his background in fine arts to help clients with their book covers. Derek believes in using art to create an immediate emotional connection with readers, and get them invested in your story before they even open the book. Check out Derek's website at:

www.creativindiecovers.com

book web publishing, ltd.

Book Web Publishing, ltd. was founded in 2000 to provide a forum for creative and unique works in children's and adult literature.

Purchase our books at www.amazon.com

Thanks!

How do you thank everyone who was part of a project that spanned nine years, seven books, and tens of thousands of photographs? It's a daunting job. If we leave anyone out please forgive us – there was an overwhelming number of people who have been part of our lives and work during the creation of the *Broken Books* series.

First, our families:

Our husbands, Richard Fink and Stuart Paltrowitz.

Our children and their children:

Russell, Laura, Mason, and Emma Fink
Adam & Blair Paltrowitz.
Darren Paltrowitz and Melissa Andreev
Shari Paltrowitz
Stacey, Greg, Johnny, and Nicky Rossi.
Meryl & Tony Waters.

Our extended families:

Harvey Fink

Robin March

Bruce and Jillian Milman

Ronnie & Sherry Milman

Dr. Sandra Roth

Barbara & Dr. Chris Woolley

Many thanks to our friends and supporters who listened to our stories, drowned our troubles in chocolate, and were always there when we needed them. Sheryl Ackerman, Jay Braiman, Dr. Barton Cohen, Sheldon Crooks, Cindy DiBiasi, Joyce & Joel Feldman, Melissa Friedman, Dr. Edward Fryman, Pat & Mary Ann Hannon, Howie Hutchinson, Janet & Rich Kam, Dale Kranz, Bill Kumar, Jerry & Jill Lash, Dr. Carol Levy, Joan Mirabella, Gail Orlick, Barbara Saks, Rachel Teplin, John Viollis, and Sandra Weiss.

Special appreciation goes to our readers: Fern Friedman, Laura & Russell Fink, Craig Oldfather, Dr. Sandra Roth – our experts: Nancy Allegretti, Phoebe Balsky, Mary Ann Hannon, Margaret Mendel, our designer, Derek Murphy, and our copy editor, Pat Hannon.

Thanks to Sue and Ken Yaeger, who generously shared their experiences and insights to bring these books alive.

Much gratitude to Tim Jaccard, AMT Children of Hope Foundation/Baby Safe Haven Program who explained his program and how important it is for all of us.

A tasty thanks to *Chocolate Works of Bellmore-Merrick, La Maison Du Chocolat,* and *Nom Wah Tea Parlor.*

Our gratitude goes to the many artists, authors, filmmakers, investigative reporters, photographers, psychologists, researchers, social workers, theorists, and videographers who informed our work, empowering us to accomplish our mission.

In loving memory of Judy Becker, Dora Eisenstein, Edna Fink, Joseph March, Gladys & Larry Milman, Ruth Roth, and Vincent Meo.

Last, but not least, thanks to our readers who joined us in this amazing journey.

Publisher's Note

www.ingramcontent.com/pod-product-compliance
Lightning Source LLC
Chambersburg PA
CBHW070600130626
46556CB00001B/224